SWIFT HAT-TRICK TRILOGY

Between Periods

A NOVELLA

HANNAH COWAN

First Edition

Cover Designed by, @booksnmoods

Edited And Proofed by, Sandra @oneloveediting

ISBN:978-1-990804-01-4

Disclaimer

Before you dive into this novella, please know that you should not read this as a standalone. Lucky Hit must be read before Between Periods in order for you to understand the characters and world. These things will not be introduced here.

Playlist

Best Fucking Summer — Atlus ♥ 3:25

Family — David Guetta, Bebe Rexha, Ty Dolla $ign, A Boogie Wit da Hoodie ♥ 2:39

If I Know Me — Morgan Wallen ♥ 2:39

Never Gonna Be Alone — Nickelback ♥ 3:47

Look After You — The Fray ♥ 4:27

Beautiful Crazy — Luke Combs ♥ 3:13

Easier — 5 Seconds Of Summer ♥ 2:37

Killing Me Slowly — Bad Wolves ♥ 3:57

Chasing After You — Ryan Hurd, Maren Morris ♥ 3:28

Medicine — ANTH, Conor Maynard ♥ 3:57

Someone To You — BANNERS ♥ 3:40

Better Man — 5 Seconds Of Summer ♥ 3:10

For my readers –

Thank you for showing these characters so much love.
This one is for you.

1

Oakley

My arm is a steel vice around Ava's waist as we board the plane to Mexico. My girlfriend practically vibrates at my side, the three fruity drinks she gulped down in the airport restaurant warming her blood and dissolving her inhibitions.

I peer down and smile at her as my heart rattles in my chest. Pride, happiness, excitement—it's all there as I watch her cheeks flush a bright shade of pink, and her green eyes shine with a potent hunger for adventure.

"I can feel you looking at me, weirdo."

She's grinning when our eyes meet. Her smile carves itself into my soul, right over the scarred outlines of where it already lives. I wear her markings with pride, wishing they were visible for everyone to see.

"You'd think you would be used to it by now."

I laugh under my breath and move her in front of me once we enter the cabin of the plane. Already having memorized our set numbers, I guide her toward the empty seats and motion for her to sit beside the window while I toss our bags above us.

It feels stuffy, too crowded for my tastes, but I swallow down the complaints and flop down beside Ava. If it were up to me, we would be on a private jet or at least be sitting in first class, but Ava brushed off my pleas and insisted we fly commercial. She thinks I've become a bit spoiled, and she wouldn't be entirely wrong. I don't even remember the last time I flew on a plane that didn't have the Seattle Seals logo etched on the seats and enough legroom for me to stretch out completely.

Speaking of legroom, I currently have none. My left knee digs into the back of the seat in front of me while the other hangs in the aisle, getting knocked by every passing passenger before I'm being glared at like I've been sitting here watching porn on full blast on my phone for the past few minutes.

There's a stifled laugh from beside me, and I whip my head to the side to see Ava smiling into a closed fist, looking everywhere but at me. Resting my palm on her exposed thigh (thank you, jean shorts) I squeeze it and grumble, "You think this is funny, do you?"

She nods, wide eyes finally flicking to my scowl. "It's nice to see you be humbled."

I pitch Ava's inner thigh and look away from her just in time to catch sight of a mess of blonde hair heading toward us. My sister skips along the aisle with a massive smile and two tall men following closely behind her.

"See! I told you we wouldn't be late," Gracie hums in satisfaction, twirling around to tap Tyler's nose before facing forward again and fixing her excited stare on me.

She ignores Tyler's glare like she always does and bounces her way over to the seats across the aisle.

"Hey, guys," Adam says from behind Tyler, wearing a typical, relaxed expression that has me lifting my hand in a small wave as a feeling of familiarity blankets my shoulders.

I don't expect much of a greeting from Tyler, not after he's been stuck babysitting my sister for the past couple of hours, so I accept his grunt as a hello without complaint. I owe both of my best friends for watching out for her after she all but refused my offer to ride with Ava and me to the airport.

Apparently, two hours is too early to be arriving at the airport before a flight in Gracie world.

There's a high-pitched growl from beside me, and I watch with an arched brow as Gracie attempts to pull her hot pink leather carry-on above her head. A string of trucker-like curses falls from her mouth when it proves too heavy. Knowing my little sister, there's most definitely enough clothes and toiletries packed inside of the bag to last her far longer than a week on the beach.

I'm pushing out of my seat as soon as her shoulders slump in defeat, ready to help, when I'm hit with a feeling of uneasiness. I suck in a harsh breath between my teeth when Tyler moves before I have the chance. He stiffly steps behind her and rips the carry-on from her grip, sliding it into the compartment nearly at his eye level before doing the same with the rest of the bags. I don't realize I've been white-knuckling the armrest until Ava slowly peels my fingers away from it and interlocks them with hers instead.

"Thank you," Gracie mumbles when she spins around to face him again, head tilted back so she's able to make eye contact. Tyler's posture is pin-straight as he stiffly nods and gestures for her to sit down. She all but tosses herself into the window seat before staring at him with raised brows. Her gaze flickers between Tyler and the seat beside her.

I look at Adam and find him already watching me. There's a question in his eyes as he waits for me to tell him what I need him to do here. Nodding once, I give him the go-ahead.

Adam slaps Tyler on the shoulder blade and brushes past him, sitting beside Gracie. "You bring any good movies, Little H?"

Maybe I should feel like an asshole for not letting my sister sit next to the guy she's been crushing on for two years—okay, maybe I do a little—but she's only eighteen.

He's too old for her. Not to mention Tyler is one of my closest friends. I know him in ways that she doesn't. They wouldn't be good together. She's too . . . *Gracie* for him.

Tyler finally turns around to move to the empty aisle seat

directly in front of me and glances at me briefly, just long enough for me to see that I've offended him before looking away.

"She's a little old for you to be scaring away boys, Oakley," Ava hums, her nails moving along the top of my hand, making me shiver.

I press a soft kiss to the top of her head and lean back against the headrest. "She'll never be too old."

Ava, ever the voice of reason, makes me feel guilt like no other as she says, "Let her have fun on this trip. You know how stressed she's been these past few weeks with her new job."

I frown because she's right. Besides the few days before her dance competitions growing up, I haven't seen my sister this worked up. Between choreographing dances for children of all ages and teaching alongside the Devil Incarnate, AKA Cleo Manford, Gracie's new boss, she's been strung tight enough I worry she'll end up snapping in half.

It's a good opportunity for her, but I know it isn't what she was looking for. My protective nature hates that there isn't anything I can do—or anything she *wants* me to do—to help her. It's my job to take care of her, but the older she gets, the harder I'm finding it to do so.

I turn to look at Gracie and smile almost instantly when I see her handing Adam one of her headphones and swiping through a bunch of pre-downloaded movies on her iPad. Adam flicks her in the cheek when she tries to play one of her Nicholas Sparks ones before he grabs the device from her altogether and starts scrolling through her endless list.

Ava squeezes my knee. "I wish you would have humoured me with the stick-on moustache."

I turn to her and crack a grin, knowing full well bringing up the disguise she insisted I wear before we left is just a ploy to distract me. It works well enough that I pull the brim of my hat down to further cover my eyes and slouch in my seat.

"Nobody has recognized me without it. Maybe I'm not as famous as I thought I was." I stick out my bottom lip but shoot my girlfriend a wink.

The fake moustache Ava brought home with her yesterday looked like a dead squirrel. There was no way in hell I was going to glue it on my face in the first place, fear of recognition or not. I would rather be forced to take a face-numbing number of selfies and sign a million autographs than have to smell some musty-ass piece of fake hair any day.

"You're lucky we didn't fly out of Seattle or Vancouver. I'm not sure we would be saying the same thing." Ava snorts, shimmying closer and resting her head against my shoulder.

We both spare a look at the burly, dark-haired man sitting directly in front of me.

Tyler entered the pros—undrafted—a few months ago, exactly a year after I did, and even though he wasn't sure anything would come from him continuing to play past his draft year, it clearly paid off. He's now a rookie defenseman for the Vancouver Warriors—my dream team.

Ava was worried that watching one of our best friends be snatched up by the team I wanted would build a rift of resentment between us, but if anything, it's done the opposite. I'm incredibly proud of Tyler and now have a fire lit under my ass to do everything I can to eventually join him over there. Hopefully, sooner rather than later.

"Worried about all the Bateman fangirls?" I laugh and kiss the top of her head, breathing in the scent of floral shampoo.

"More like the Hutton ones," she grumbles. "Remember the one that ripped the hat off of your head last week and then begged you to sign it for her? I mean, seriously?"

An uncomfortable feeling slithers up my spine. The urge to touch my head and search for the small spot of missing hair an inch above my left ear is a strong one. At least the mall security guard was close by and able to escort the girl far, *far* away from me before Ava slapped her.

Clasping a hand around Ava's thigh, I say, "Put all those

memories in storage for the next week, baby. This trip is all about us."

Once preseason training finishes and the season begins, life will start moving at lightning speed again. We need this time together now. While we still have it. Lord knows when we'll get another chance to spend a week away on the beach with our best friends.

I feel her nod and loop her arm through mine, pressing herself tight against me, as close as she can get with the armrest pinched between us. I'm close to telling her how much more comfortable it would have been in first class when her next words silence me.

"I love you, Oakley."

My chest swells at the familiar saying that I can't see myself ever getting used to hearing from her. "I love you too, sweetheart."

2

Gracie

I CAN ALREADY FEEL THE ALCOHOL WARMING MY BLOOD and bringing a flush to my neck and cheeks. The pool water is a few degrees warmer than I was hoping as it hits my upper stomach in soft waves.

It's only been a few hours since we arrived in Cancún, Mexico, but I couldn't wait to get out and explore the resort once I made it to my room. Based on how luxurious it is, I must owe Oakley thousands of dollars for my stay. Not like he would let me pay him back. My brother's love language is definitely acts of service.

A group of guys who look similar in age to the ones I arrived here with is lined up along the edge of the pool, chatting and slinging back pee-coloured frothy liquid in plastic cups.

I noticed them as soon as I slid in the water and finished the remainder of my strawberry daiquiri. That was not even five minutes ago. Since then, I haven't been able to ignore the looks of interest that have spread across several of their faces. It's not like they've been subtle about their attraction to me either. The spiky-haired blond third from the end has been leaning forward past his buddies to sneak a glance at me more than a few times.

Growing up dancing, I've never found myself to be overly

self-conscious. My body has been worked to the max for far too long to ignore the tight, thick muscles of my abdomen and thighs or the generous lift of my backside. Nevertheless, I've never appreciated being gawked at like a piece of meat by alcohol-guzzling men.

Crouching just enough that the water reaches my collarbones, I set my empty cup down on the edge of the pool and move my arms in front of me, spreading my fingers to allow the water to move between them. It's noisy, conversations taking place close by and the sound of bare feet clapping on the pool deck. The speakers above the bar behind me play a familiar song, and I hum along, closing my eyes.

I'm not sure how long I stay in the same spot, back pressed to the pool tile and basking in the sun, but when I open my eyes again, the group of men has been replaced with a rigid, bare-chested Tyler. A beautifully half-naked, *wet* Tyler, who's glaring at me with eyes dark enough to send a shiver up my spine.

Swallowing hard, I reach up to fiddle with the scrunchie holding my hair up and smile. Desire pools low in my belly, and my chest begins to ache, my heart skipping beats. My body's reaction to him is expected but not welcomed. Not when he's looking at me like he wants to throw my ass in the ocean and feed me to a shark.

His sharp jaw clenches, lips in a tight line, but I don't let my smile drop. It grows instead as I wave him over and smack the edge of the pool beside me. "Stop glaring at me, Ty. You're making everyone nervous."

He quirks a brow, and I swear his mouth twitches like he wants to smile. My heart soars when he rolls his eyes and stalks toward me. His tall, fit body slices through the water with a confidence that has my thighs pressing together.

"You should have waited for everyone else before you went off alone," he grumbles.

Even though he stays far enough away to leave a generous amount of space still between us, his presence crowds me.

"I suppose it was you that scared off my admirers?" The thought makes me happier than it probably should, but I cover my interest with another question. "Did my brother send you after me?"

Tyler shakes his head with a brief grunt and moves closer, still leaving lots of breathing room between us. He wants to keep a safe space between him and the obsessed fan, AKA me, I'm guessing. Embarrassment coils like barbed wire in my stomach.

It isn't a secret by any means that I've spent the past couple of years crushing on one of my brother's best friends, but the more Tyler treats me like a kid with a case of chicken pox that he doesn't want to catch, the more I wish it was.

"I'm not going to maul you in front of the entire resort. It was just a silly schoolgirl crush. Get over it. I am."

I'm being immature, but it doesn't embarrass me as much as feeling like a groupie does.

That stupid bushy eyebrow of his lifts again, and I get the urge to lunge forward and slap it back down. Tyler places a palm on the edge of the pool and leans his weight against it, drawing my eyes to his biceps as they bulge and strain from the effort. My mouth feels dry, the moisture disappearing as my tongue pokes the inside of my cheek.

Humour lights up his stare, and he smirks, knowing full well that he's succeeded in proving his point.

I am still very much into Tyler Bateman. And I'm a bold-faced liar if I say otherwise.

I watch the water ripple as he takes two steps toward me, close enough now that I can see the usual barely there hair on his jaw is missing.

"It's cute, Gray. But it can't ever happen. You know that."

He's only half-right. I know that *he* believes it can't happen, but I don't. While I may be young, I'm not naïve nor blind to the way he's started to watch me when he thinks I'm not looking.

As if to prove my own point, I fiddle with the strap of my bikini top and swipe my tongue across my bottom lip. My blood begins to sizzle beneath my skin when his stare grows heated and falls on my mouth and then to my collarbone, where I have my strap pulled tight between two fingers, before drifting to the swell of my breasts.

"No, Ty. I don't," I say, suddenly breathless when I see the hand that was once pressed flat to the pool deck curl into a fist. "But if it will make you happy, I'll let you keep living in denial a little while longer."

A deep rumble grows in his chest when I close the space between us and lean up on my tiptoes, grazing my mouth across his jaw. His breath hitches when my hot breath hits his skin, and I whisper, "I'll save you a seat at dinner."

And with that, I'm backing away and walking out of the pool, a set of coffee-brown eyes burning holes into my back.

ADAM CURSES at someone on the phone loud enough that the guests at the tables closest to us scowl in our direction. An older man with a very unfortunate receding hairline and a beer belly that hangs from beneath his button-up hisses something I don't catch and throws up his middle finger.

I have to stifle my laugh with my hand when Adam shows him his middle finger in return, and Oakley says something along the lines of, "Yeah, okay, Homer Simpson."

The breeze from the air-conditioning in the buffet-style restaurant we opted to eat at tonight feels amazing on my bare shoulders. I toy with the dewy glass just recently topped up with water in front of me and smile.

"What's got you so happy, Gray?" Oakley asks, a look of pure joy in his eyes.

He has to be feeling the same way that I am. Like we've found something so rare in this group of people that we can hardly believe it's real life. How did we get lucky enough to be surrounded by so much love and support? It's a dream, honestly.

"I'm just glad I came," I answer honestly. "I'm happy I was even invited in the first place."

Ava scoffs and reaches across the table to flick me in the upper arm. "Don't be ridiculous. You're just as much a part of this family as any of us."

The term *family* has my belly filling with warmth. "Please don't make me cry on vacation. I consider that a sin."

Oakley leans back in his chair and rests his arm on the back of Ava's. He tosses me a grin so wide I can't help but return it with one of my own. There was a time when I didn't know if I would ever see my brother smile like this again.

"I also consider crying on vacation a sin," Adam says, joining the conversation again from the seat beside me. His phone is tucked away now, and the frustration that twisted his features just minutes prior is long gone.

"Taking phone calls on vacation is also highly frowned upon," Ava pokes, her curiosity obvious.

Her interest is not surprising by any means, considering how close the two of them are. There's probably nobody who knows Adam better than Ava does.

I watch with interest as Adam clicks his tongue in mock annoyance and shoves a hand through his spiked brown hair. "I already turned it off, Mom."

"Everything is okay, right?" she asks calmly.

Adam nods and flashes her a megawatt smile, one that would have melted my panties on the spot if I were a normal eighteen-year-old not already crushing on someone else.

"Look who decided to join us," my brother says, looking over my head.

I feel his presence press against my back before I hear a pair of sneakers thumping on the floor. Flicking my eyes across the table at Ava, I see her lips twitch, like she's trying not to smile as she alternates between looking at me and the giant man coming up to the table.

"Sorry. I passed out and forgot to set an alarm." Tyler's voice is gruff, raspy. It brings goosebumps to my skin and collars my throat so that I can't speak. "Buffet, yeah? I hope you weren't waiting for me."

The brave girl from the pool, the one who demanded the attention of the guy she wanted, has retreated far, far back in my body like the traitor she is. I'm left with a cotton-mouthed, leg shaking, nervous little girl instead. It's embarrassing.

I nearly forgot about the empty chair to my right, so when it pulls out with a loud screeching sound, I jolt in surprise. The tablecloth becomes the most interesting thing in the restaurant when Tyler sits down beside me and pushes himself closer to the table.

"Gracie insisted that it was rude to eat without everyone here," Ava says slyly, earning herself a glare when I look up from the table.

I feel Tyler's eyes burning into the side of my face as I try desperately to ignore him. It seems impossible to keep up my act when the breeze from the AC sends a cloud of his cologne straight to me. There's a snicker from somewhere at the table that I ignore as I shoot out of my seat.

"Everyone's here now. Let's eat. I'm starving." My words are rushed, and I'm clearly out of breath, but I choose to ignore those things and focus on making it to the buffet tables before I implode instead.

There's no way that I would ever, *ever* get over that level of embarrassment in this lifetime or the next.

3

Gracie

I SLIP MY ROUNDED SUNGLASSES BACK OVER MY EYES and lean against one of the many colourful lounge chairs spread out along the infinity pool. The sun is hot against my tanning-oil-lathered pale skin, making the frozen drink in my hand more noticeable as it melts into a slushy.

Ava gave me a hard time about using such a hefty amount of tanning oil before I left her room, considering I burn even under a thick layer of SPF, and tanning lotion *probably* isn't the smartest choice to avoid that. But if there's one thing I'm going to get on this trip, it's a freaking tan.

It's just after lunchtime, and the resort is packed full of bikini-clad women and shirtless men. A sight I can't say isn't the least bit enjoyable.

Back in Vancouver, the guys are either wearing white tees with rolled sleeves and chinos, or fancy business suits that have short-legged pants to show off their ugly socks covered with pot leaves. I much prefer glistening washboard abs and brightly coloured swim trunks.

The five of us have been in Mexico for just over a day now, leaving me with only five days left to drink as many complimentary alcoholic beverages as possible and kiss as many random half-naked beach bums as it takes to forget about all of my petty problems back home.

It had been way too freaking hard to convince my new boss to let me take this week off, so I think I deserve not to worry about a damn thing for a few days.

When I first started working for Cleo at her small dance studio in downtown Van, I half expected to spend my days standing off to the side as an extra in case she needed someone to cover for her or help the odd kid remember a missed step. I didn't expect her to throw all of the choreography for our upcoming recitals onto me.

I'm not new to the world of dance or to creating my own routines. I've been a dancer for all my life, for Pete's sake. But until now, I've never had to come up with a complete performance, top to bottom, for someone else, let alone multiple little ones with overly involved parents ready with their pitchforks freshly sharpened in case I embarrass their children.

I know that I should be looking at the situation in a more positive light, considering it will give me experience with something I've never done before. But the stress from the bucketload of new responsibilities is already building up, and with my unwanted anxiety rearing its ugly head whenever possible, it seems like more of a chore than a learning opportunity.

"You couldn't have worn a bathing suit with a bit more fabric?" I hear Oakley ask as he comes up on my left and sits in an empty chair. "What kind of bathing suit is that, anyway?"

Ava follows shortly after, a large sun hat flopping in her eyes and an adorable white one-piece with criss-crossed straps covering her lean body.

"Leave her alone, babe." She swats his arm and flops down on his lap. Oakley wraps an arm around her middle and pulls her closer to his chest. "I think she looks beautiful."

I grin. "And that's why you're my favourite." Wiping the

beads of sweat from my forehead, I look at the crowds of people in the pool and ask, "What took you guys so long? I'm going to burn if I stay out here for much longer."

"It's better if you don't know," Oakley says smugly, a smirk on his lips, no doubt. I don't look to find out for sure.

Ava snorts when I scrunch my face in disgust. "I told you not to put so much oil on. Been there, done that, Gray."

She reaches into the large bag she set beside her chair and pulls out a pair of sunglasses and a bottle of sunscreen. She slides her sunglasses on and holds the sunscreen toward Oakley. "Heads up."

As my brother reaches forward to grab the bottle, a stray hand pushes him away and swipes the sunscreen.

"Thanks, Ava. I left mine upstairs," Tyler teases. He joins the group with a beautifully rare and relaxed grin. The same one that never fails to awaken the family of butterflies in my stomach.

Oakley scoffs and shoots his elbow back, hitting Tyler above the band of his swim trunks. A pained groan slips from his lips, and I become way too easily distracted by the hand rubbing at the two deep lines leading to what hides beneath his trunks.

"Asshole," Tyler mutters and smacks the back of Oakley's head on his way to the empty chair beside mine.

Coincidence? Maybe. *Maybe not.*

I immediately look away and chew on my lip, praying that nobody caught the eggplant emojis in my eyes just now. Oakley would have a field day with that. I probably wouldn't see another day outside of my hotel room.

The legs of the chair squeak as Tyler sits down. I peek over at him to find him watching me, his head tilted and the ghost of a grin tugging on his lips.

"You know, if I wasn't such a confident guy, your staring would have made me self-conscious."

The teasing whisper has my eyes bulging as I gulp air like a fish out of water.

"I wasn't staring," I argue.

He arches a brow and leans toward me, elbows resting on his knees, his fingers mere inches from my thigh. "No? Because I was."

I twist in my seat and stare at him open-mouthed.

"Pink is your colour," he murmurs. His eyes trail over my skin, and goosebumps follow.

"I didn't know I had a colour. I thought I looked good in everything."

My heart thumps against my rib cage the second his eyes meet mine. His eyes hold mine for a few seconds before his gaze falls somewhere else. *Dismissed*.

I empty my lungs and sneak a look at my brother and Ava. They're completely locked in their own world. Neither of them is paying any attention to us.

"Are you searching for another compliment, Gray? Because I'm all out." He turns to face me again, his mouth set in a tight line. He spreads his legs wider, and the urge to get up and stand between them swims to the surface.

"I don't need one." I shrug. "There's already so many written across your face. Now, if you'll excuse me, I have to get out of this sun before I combust."

I stand confidently and immediately feel a rush of pride for not letting Tyler get the better of me like I usually do.

Turning my back to him, I reach down and grab my beach bag, smirking when I hear the sharp intake of breath behind me. Sliding my bag to rest on my shoulder, I tighten my ponytail before looking back and raising my brow.

"You know, if I wasn't such a confident girl, your staring would have made me self-conscious."

Tyler

I SLAM back another drink and scold myself for being reckless enough to flirt with Gracie not even ten feet from her brother —*my best friend*.

The sun has set now, and the pool deck is otherwise empty except for the odd cleaning person walking around or myself, calf-deep in the chlorinated water.

A bottle of tequila sits in my closed palm, providing me with a sense of burning comfort every time I tilt it back and swallow. I know there are other ways to deal with my feelings, but none are as easy as letting the thoughts get completely washed away by a wave of clear liquid.

When I saw Gracie sitting by the pool with Oakley and Ava earlier, I was tempted to pick her up and carry her back to my room. That tiny triangle bikini top that barely covered the tits that seemed to have grown overnight and the matching bottoms that tied on the side—so easy to undo—made my cock stiffer than a fucking wooden board. I nearly put a towel over my crotch.

I don't know what caused the sudden urge, but I wanted to slip one of my T-shirts over her toned stomach and carry her away to my room more than I wanted air to breathe.

She isn't the nervous, word-vomiting teenage girl she used to be back when I would come over for Anne's famous lasagna or to practice shooting with Oakley in his backyard.

No.

Time had changed more than just her brother and me. It had changed her too. In all the right places.

I know she's struggling with work and Anne's recent health struggles. I know that her dipshit of an ex-boyfriend dumped her on a limb and that she pretends not to be hurt by it.

There isn't a day that Oakley doesn't talk about his sister. He misses her—living in a different country and all—and doesn't miss a chance to gush about how proud of her he is or how badly he wishes he could have been there to shove that dweeb's face into a brick wall.

Right now, I hate that I'm treated like a part of their family. I hate that at this very moment, my dick is on high alert, tenting the crotch of my basketball shorts just thinking about Gracie Hutton.

I gulp down another swig of tequila and scrunch my face as it tears down my throat, leaving it raw. Grunting, I let my neck go limp and close my eye, kicking my feet in the water.

"The pool closed an hour ago."

"Fuck," I mutter under my breath and set the bottle down off to the side a little firmer than necessary. "Then what are you doing here?" I ask, louder than before.

I force my eyes to open and lift my head so I can stare at the last person I need to see tonight.

Gracie wears light blue jean shorts with a rip in the front pocket and a yellow tank top as she stands a few feet away with her arms crossed. She lifts a curious brow but smiles slightly, almost knowingly. The idea that she knows more about me than I want her to pisses me off.

"Same as you. I needed to think."

She sits down on the edge of the pool beside me but doesn't relax her tense shoulders until after a few beats when I still haven't told her to get lost.

"You don't know me."

"Don't I?"

I ponder her question as if I care about the answer.

"Go sit by yourself if you need to think. This spot is taken," I grumble, too tired to put up a real fight. I'm not going to admit it, especially not to her, but her company isn't all bad.

"Here's good," she chimes, smiling a megawatt smile that nearly knocks me into the pool.

She used to have braces; I've seen the old pictures of her in middle school that hang on the staircase at her mother's house. They paid off, big-time. Her teeth are perfectly straight and so white that she could be in a Whitestrips commercial. I drop my blurred gaze to my knees, itching for a smoke.

"Your loss. I'm not exactly the best company," I grunt.

"Who said that? Whoever did was a tool. I think you're pretty great company." She sounds so sure, so sincere, that it makes my stomach churn.

I squint my eyes at her before I can stop myself. Gracie giggles in response, moving her feet in slow circles in the water. Her hands are spread out behind her, and she leans back on them, tilting her head back and letting her hair swing along her back.

"I mean, you're not *always* the best company." She laughs again, meeting my stare. The twinkle of the string lights hung above us reflects in her blue eyes. "You can be a real asshole."

It's my turn to laugh. "Yeah, I can."

She doesn't reply this time, just looks away and gnaws on her bottom lip. Something is bothering her, but I'm too stubborn to ask what it is. So instead, I guess and mumble, "Jason was never going to be able to keep up with you, Gray. He was a fucking loser."

Her lip slips from between her teeth. "His name is Jacob."

"Jason, Jacob." I roll my eyes. "Either way. He was mediocre, amateur at best. We both know you need someone better. Someone who isn't going to tell all his friends how good you are in bed and all the things you can do with your tongue. A real man would want to keep that shit to himself, to fantasize about when you're not together and he thinks about you in bed with his hand around his cock."

Her eyes widen in surprise before she gulps a few times as though she's struggling to breathe. Fuck, I wasn't supposed to know that, was I? Great, now Oakley's going to punch me for spewing out secrets.

"Is that what I need? A real man?" she asks slowly, almost in a whisper. Her eyes bore into mine, gripping onto them with claws out.

I force myself to look away. "It's what you deserve."

And that man's not me.

It's about time we both remembered that.

4

Ava

There was a time when I thought my life was in a perpetual downward spiral. Like I had my head shoved inside a toilet while the world kept flushing me down no matter how loud I screamed or how hard I fought back.

There was no light left at the end of the tunnel, and if by some miracle there was, I wouldn't have been able to see it past my shattered vision and hatred of the world around me.

That was years ago now. Back before I knew what it felt like to be held in a mother's arms and kissed by a man who would move mountains for me. I've learned that the bad doesn't necessarily disappear once you've become accustomed to the good, but it sure does help drown it out.

Still, there are times when the darkness shadows the light, and you fall back into the pit of despair that you've only recently climbed out of. For me, that happens when I'm the happiest, when I'm full of so much love, pride, and excitement that the fear of losing everything becomes a weight too heavy to bear, forcing me back into my protective shell.

Right now, here in paradise with the most important people to me, is exactly one of those times.

A low rumble sounds in my ear, and a large hand smooths the

exposed skin on my waist. I release a sigh, shutting my eyes in the darkened room.

It's been a couple of hours since Oakley and I returned to our room and headed to bed after dinner, but I haven't slept, too caught up on the feelings threatening to burst inside my chest like an overfilled balloon. There's the slightest slip of orange spilling from beneath the blinds, so I can't have been awake for too long.

"Are you okay, baby?" Oakley's words brush my ear and neck, making me shiver. That large hand slides to my stomach as he pulls me closer, my back stuck to his hard stomach.

"I thought you were asleep."

"Something's bothering you," he states while pressing his lips to my pulse point and humming in satisfaction.

I place my hand on the one splayed across my stomach and squeeze. "I'm okay."

There's a grumble before he shifts us, moving to hover above me, two thick arms on either side of my head.

"Try again."

He stares down at me with an unguarded expression that has my breath catching.

"It's been two years. You'd think I would be used to you looking at me like that by now."

Oakley's laugh fills my belly with warmth as he shakes above me. White teeth beam when he grins, pink lips stretched wide. "I'm glad I still have that effect on you, beautiful. It will be a cold day in hell when you don't make me feel the exact same way."

Sucking in a slow, calming breath, I press my palm to his jaw and say, "I'm just feeling very happy, and that makes me nervous. It's like I'm still waiting for the other shoe to drop." For everything to come crashing down on me, burying me alive underneath a pile of hopes and dreams.

Expecting disappointment is incredibly suffocating. It's a feeling that lingers in your soul like cigarette smoke on your favourite sweater.

"There aren't any shoes dropping, Ava. This life, this feeling of contentment and belonging? That's how you should have felt every single day for the past twenty-one years. You were dealt an awful hand, but the game is over now. You get to walk away with the jackpot. You're mine, and I don't plan on ever letting you feel that way again."

The confidence and determination in Oakley's words create a lump in my throat that I can't seem to swallow down. When my eyes begin to burn and water, I know there's no stopping the tears before they fall.

Thumbs swipe each tear away. "It kills me to see you cry."

A laugh bubbles in my chest. "I barely ever cry anymore. You can thank yourself for that."

"I would do anything to keep your eyes free from tears forever, baby."

Lips press to mine in a deep, full kiss. The energy between us shifts and coils, pulling me closer to him as my back arches and my breasts brush Oakley's chest.

Slipping my hands around his neck, I thread my fingers into the soft hair at his nape and tug him closer, so overwhelmed with the need to have him as close to me as possible. Oakley's tongue slides across my lips, parting them with a rough groan that I feel in my curled toes.

"I fucking love you." His words are as rough as sandpaper but warm enough to thaw an iceberg.

"I love you too."

I laugh when his lips slide to my jaw and pepper it with kisses. The day-old stubble of what once used to be a burly beard tickles the sensitive skin before I slide my hands to his bare chest and push. "You need to either shave or let your beard grow out again. This in-between is such a mood killer."

Our eyes meet again when he pulls his face from my neck and stares down at me with a look of fake outrage. His pupils are dilated, leaving only a small green ring around the edges that twinkles with mischief and a silent challenge. A large, strong hand drags down his jaw.

"A mood killer? Shall we see if it has the same effect when it's rubbing the inside of your thighs?"

I flush. "You just want me to have to walk around the resort tomorrow with a beard burn."

He cocks a brow, grinning. "And if I did?"

My thighs lift to wrap around his hips and squeeze. I can feel him hard against my stomach. "Then who am I to tell you no?"

Oakley's eyes dilate again as something predatory slithers inside them. The heat flaring from his stare has desire pooling low in my belly.

His smirk is carnal as he grabs my thighs and detaches them from his waist, pushing them open on the bed, exposing my wet panties. Once he's sure I'm not going to fight him by closing them, he pushes my baggy shirt up and off my body before tossing it to the corner of the room.

With a tight, rough sound of approval, he moves his way down my body. His mouth finds my chest, and his tongue slashes the swell of my right breast before moving to the left, sucking it hard enough for my back to arch.

"No marks, you caveman. I have to wear a bathing suit all week," I plead, albeit half-heartedly. Oakley has never held back when it comes to staking his claim on me any way he can. I love that about him, and he knows it.

There's a subtle quirk of his brow before his teeth meet my skin, nipping just hard enough to make me gasp from the sting. "It's because you're wearing a bathing suit all week that I have to mark you."

With a roll of my eyes, I slip my fingers through the overgrown curls hanging in his face, pushing them back and out of the way. Green eyes claim mine at the same time he takes my hard nipple between his lips, sucking and flicking the peak with his hot tongue.

My hips roll and lift, seeking the feeling of him more and more as my underwear becomes so slick it sticks to my swollen flesh. I clutch his shoulders beneath sweaty palms and hold him against me.

His laugh vibrates against my nipple before he lets it go with a *pop* and grins up at me, so incredibly proud of himself for turning me into a puddle of need. I glare when he shakes his head, grinning slyly and moving down to rest between my legs.

I suck in a sharp breath the second his fingers brush my center, the touch so gentle and teasing that I swallow back a growl. "Oakley."

"Yes, Ava?" My panties are pulled to the side, and he hisses, looking from my wet flesh up at me with dark, lustful eyes. "You're so beautiful."

My eyes roll into the back of my head when he spreads me open for him and swipes his tongue through my wetness.

"Jesus." His words heat my blood, bringing it to a boil. My nipples pull tight, beginning to ache without his touch, but the feeling pales in comparison to the one sparking between my hips.

"Yes," I sigh, digging my fingers deeper into his hair, scratching at his scalp.

Oakley slides a finger inside me and sucks my clit between his lips, moaning in a way that has me jolting off the bed.

There's a sound coming from somewhere in the room that sounds a lot like banging, but I'm far too lost in my own lustful haze to pay much attention to it. Until I hear Gracie's voice, that is.

Hearing your boyfriend's little sister's voice when he has his tongue in your pussy is the equivalent of having a bucket of ice water dumped on your head.

"Open the door! Lee, I lost my room key!"

I gasp when a growl vibrates against my core seconds before Oakley leans back and wipes the back of his hand across his lips. Frustration is etched on every inch of his face, making him look older than he is.

"I'm going to kill her," he says.

I crawl back underneath the blankets, my cheeks thumping with embarrassment.

There's really no reason to feel embarrassed. I'm aware that we weren't doing anything wrong, but there's no convincing myself of that at this moment in time.

A few seconds later, I hear the door open and voices blend together.

"What do you mean you lost the second one? It's the first night here, Gracie."

"I didn't mean to! I think it's in the poo—" Gracie's words are interrupted by a high-pitched hiccup that makes me smile. "Pool. You have the extra one, right? Give it to me."

Oakley scoffs loudly. "Give it to you? So you can lose it again? No way. Let me get dressed so I can walk your drunk ass back to your room."

"I can take myself, Dad."

"Don't start, Gracie. How much have you had to drink, anyway? Did you go back out alone? Dressed like this?" Silence follows his question. "Come on, Gracie. You're lucky you weren't snatched up by some creep looking for a young blonde bride."

Gracie snorts. "You're insane."

"Wait here. Don't move." The door closes before Oakley starts rooting through his suitcase.

"You can turn the light on so you can see," I say, pushing up on my elbows.

"It's fine, baby. Go to sleep, I'll be back in a few minutes." He slides on a random pair of pants and a T-shirt before moving to stand beside the bed and bending down to kiss me.

The kiss only lasts a few seconds, but it's long enough for me to taste his frustration.

"Be quick. I love you."

"I love you. Stay on your side of the bed," he teases. I laugh in response as he leaves again, this time herding Gracie back into the hallway.

I let out a long breath and roll to my side, curling up under the blankets and falling asleep easily. I'm barely jostled from my dreamless sleep when Oakley joins me again, pulling me onto his chest and wrapping me up in his arms, telling me he loves me.

And when I wake in the morning, I smile because neither of us dared to move all night.

5

Tyler

THERE'S SOMETHING DIGGING INTO MY BACK. Something sharp and annoying as fuck. Almost like one of those long, manicured fingernails that belong to my best friend's little sister.

With a rumble vibrating my chest, I lift my face from my towel on the beach and face my guest. A scowl twists my mouth when I see the fiery blonde sitting cross-legged beside me, her ass cheeks parked in the sand. She grins when she notices me looking at her.

A wave of protectiveness blasts through me as I take in her bathing suit—or lack thereof. Two triangles of neon yellow material barely contain her breasts, the swells of them spilling over the top and sides. Her bikini bottom is just as stringy, with two knots hanging on her hips, holding it up. Who knows how much of her bare ass is touching the sand.

It's even worse than the bikini she wore yesterday, and I didn't think that was possible.

"What are you wearing?" I hiss, tearing my eyes away from all of that smooth, blemish-free skin.

It's hard to focus on anything else when Gracie Hutton is nearby. She's a beaming light that I can't help but be drawn to, even when I have to remind myself just how dangerous it is to think that way about her.

The beach is pretty quiet today. Only a few vacationers are spread out on lounge chairs in the sand, not scared of the sweltering sun beating down on us, baking shoulders and noses until they're bright red. My exposed back has been hot for a while now, but I won't be getting up anytime soon. Not now, when my cock is rock hard and trying to rip a hole in my board shorts.

"A bikini," Gracie replies.

I shove my face back in my towel. My next words are muffled. "You're practically naked."

"There are girls wearing far less on this beach. I'm sure you've noticed them. I know for a fact they've noticed you."

The potent jealousy in her words makes me laugh. She makes a noise in her throat before flicking me in the ear. I don't react to the pain, opting to laugh harder instead, just to piss her off.

Gracie has made her little crush painfully obvious over the past two years, regardless of the lack of romantic progress she has and *will ever* make with me. It's not going to happen, but it would be a lie to say I didn't find it flattering.

Not only is she completely off limits because of my relationship with her brother, but she's not my type in the slightest.

Peeling my face from my towel again, I look around the beach and spot a group of girls huddled together a few yards away. They're all turned in my direction and doing an awful job of playing down their interest. I nod toward them. "Those girls?"

"They've been pointing over here since before I sat down," Gracie replies.

"Think they know who I am?"

She snorts. "No. They would already be over here if they did."

"I'm surprised you haven't gone over there and told them off yet. It usually doesn't take this long for you to try and piss all over me like a dog marking its territory."

Her cheeks flush as she drops her eyes to her bare toes,

studying them like they might detach and crawl away. A brief sting of regret singes my stomach at her hurt expression.

"Sorry." I wince. "You didn't deserve that."

She waves me off before pushing herself to a stand and frantically brushing away the sand that clings to her skin. "No, I did. That's exactly what I tend to do."

Shit. Panic has me on my feet before she has a chance to take off. I grab her wrist and shiver at the tingle in my fingertips. "I'm sorry, Gray. I don't want this week to be awkward between us."

Her eyes are wide as she looks at the hand holding her before sliding them to my naked chest. I swallow hard when her baby blue eyes glaze over with a sheen of arousal as they continue to move along my body, snagging on the fabric that hides my throbbing cock. Suddenly the vast length of the beach feels too intimate of a place to be alone with her.

I drop her wrist like it's burned my fingertips and take a step back with wobbly knees. She's blinking slowly, looking half in a daze when I say, "I'm going to head back."

"Okay," she mumbles.

"Don't stay here alone wearing that, Gracie. I'm serious."

"Unless you plan on being the one to take me back to my room and dress me in something else, keep your comments to yourself," she snarks.

She pins me in place with a sharp glare before flicking her blonde curls over her shoulder and taking off toward the water, leaving me in the dust. I suck in a pained breath as I stare at her, my fingers curling into fists.

Only a small triangle of yellow fabric sits at the lowest point of her back, the rest of the bikini bottom sitting snugly in the crack of her ass, leaving the curved flesh completely exposed.

"Jesus Christ." Tipping my head back, I place my hands on my waist and release a pained groan. I try to remind myself that it doesn't matter what she's wearing. That it's not my problem. That it would be a good thing for her to catch someone else's attention while we're here, but each thought only pisses me off more, to the point I can no longer keep myself from going after her.

"Wait!" I shout. My toes dig into the sand as I jog down the beach, closing the distance between us before she even makes it to the water.

Gracie whips around to face me when I grab her wrist again. Fuck, her skin is soft.

"You are aggravating," she hisses, her face all scrunched up.

"Me?" I bark a laugh. "You're the one running around half-naked. Not to mention *alone*. Do you have any idea how good you look right now? There isn't a guy on this fucking beach that isn't wondering what he has to do to get you alone."

Her eyes flare as she takes a step closer to me. Our chests are only inches apart, both of us breathing heavily.

"What about you? Is that what you're thinking too?"

I grind my jaw. I've opened that door, and now she isn't going to back down until I either give her what she wants or crush her spirit. Neither are ideal options.

My stare falls to her mouth as her tongue slowly runs across her bottom lip, leaving it wet. A rumble builds in my chest that I let escape. If she knew half of the things running through my mind right now, she wouldn't stop poking until my control was nothing more than a pile of ashes at her feet.

"No," I rasp, closing the gap between our bodies. "I'm thinking far worse things than they are, Gracie. And I'm telling you right now not to provoke me."

She gasps, making her hardened nipples brush my chest. I swallow a moan at the sudden feel of her against me.

Her body shouldn't feel this good, so soft and breakable. Alarms are blaring in my head, but they become muffled when her fingertips brush the back of my hand. The contact is a zap to my nerves that I wasn't expecting. And when she drags her fingers up my arm and wraps them around my bicep, more of my willpower shatters.

"But what if I want to provoke you? What would you do

about it?" she whispers. Her eyelashes flutter as she peers up at me with feigned innocence.

I grab her by the nape and tangle my fingers in her hair. With lust warming my blood, I pull her face close to mine. Her pupils grow when my words brush her lips.

"I would take you back to my room and fuck you hard enough you wouldn't be able to leave."

6

Gracie

"WHAT?" I'M SO BREATHLESS MY WORDS ARE whispered.

My thighs are slick, and when I rub them together, a friction builds in my core that has my head turning foggy. I'm terrified to look down and see a wet spot on my bikini.

Tyler's breaths are hot angry puffs on my mouth. I run my tongue along my lips, like I'm trying to taste him and not fight the dryness. His eyes flare as he watches me, a gravelly moan falling between us.

"But you'd like that, wouldn't you?" he asks. His nose brushes mine, the feel of his lips on my cheek making my head swim. "You want it so bad that your tight little pussy is dripping for me. Isn't it, Gracie?" *Oh God.* "But it shouldn't, because you know I can't touch you like that."

I whimper, and suddenly, it doesn't matter that we're on the beach, standing too close, touching too comfortably. Tyler has managed to play my body in a way that's shut down my common sense. And I can't get enough of it.

With a brave step, I'm pressing my body flush against his. Hot, hard skin meets mine, and I fight to keep my eyes from rolling into the back of my head.

"Gracie," he warns, the guttural tone of his voice making my nipples ache against the thin fabric of my top. His hips flex, and his hard cock pushes against my lower stomach. "Tell me what you want me to do. *Now*."

I blink in surprise. There's a determination in his eyes that he seems to be fighting.

Forcing a swallow, I reach up and circle his wrists before tugging and releasing his fingers from my hair. His jaw works as I hold his stare, reveling in the power I feel watching him fighting to keep himself under control. I keep his fingers pressed to my skin but drag them to my front, to my collarbone and then further, to the valley between my breasts. A rumble builds in his chest, lust blowing his pupils.

"But you are touching me like that, Tyler."

He spreads his fingers until they cover the swell of my breasts. "But I shouldn't."

"Nobody has to know. Just us." *Don't stop.*

"I can't touch you like this out here. Not on this beach where everyone can see," he grunts. His fingertips press deeper.

I push up on my toes and hover my mouth over his jaw. He smells like aftershave and sunscreen, and I breathe him in.

"Then take me to your room. Please, Tyler." I plant my hands on his chest and fall back on my feet. There's a battle raging in his eyes, one that tells me he needs me to be the one to push. To be the one who carries the burden of our decision, and I will without hesitation.

I tighten my grip on his wrists and, with a steadying breath, move his left hand over my chest, down my stomach, and to the thin waistband of my bikini bottoms. A shiver rushes through me when he toys with the fabric, not making a move to slip beneath it.

He sucks his bottom lip into his mouth and bites down hard on it before I risk a glance around the beach. The group of girls from earlier is turned away from us, but there's a part of me that wouldn't care if they did see what I'm about to do. The beach around us is otherwise unoccupied. My heart flip-flops in my chest.

Tightening my grip on his hand, I urge it lower and lower, until his fingertips bump my swollen clit and meet the wetness that's soiled my bikini bottoms. I gasp at the contact, shuddering into his chest as he mutters a rough "*Fuck*."

"Tyler," I whimper.

He leans his face close to mine, turns his body slightly to the side to block our hands from view, and watches me with fire in his eyes as he drags his fingers down my pussy. I bite my tongue when he cups me in his palm and hooks his thumb under the side of my bikini, moving it out of the way. My mouth gapes when two fingers slip through my wetness.

Tyler presses his forehead to mine, and he swirls a finger around my opening. "Is this all for me?"

My walls pulse, the unfiltered want in his voice acting like a conductor to the electricity building in my veins. "You know it is."

I whimper in protest when he removes his hand. "Wha—"

A full-body shudder works through me as he lifts his fingers to his mouth and slides them between his lips, tasting me.

His eyes narrow, igniting with something dangerous, maybe even feral, as he says, "Let's go."

I SQUEAL when Tyler throws me on the bed and climbs over me, holding my body in place between his knees. My chest rises and falls rapidly at a pace that should feel concerning but isn't in the slightest.

"You're gorgeous," Tyler mumbles. His eyes slide down my body, leaving a trail of fire in their wake. "I don't want to tarnish you."

I frown, shaking my head. "You couldn't."

Thick black brows tug together between two dark, guarded eyes. Tyler's jaw works as he stares down at me, and I would do anything to know what he's thinking. What he wants to say but won't.

I reach behind my neck and slowly pull one string of my bikini, untying the knot. Then I bring both strings forward and drop them on my chest. Placing my palms on the crumpled hotel sheets, I lift my chin and arch my back, offering myself to the man I've wanted so badly for years.

I expected him to dive right in, to pull the tiny triangles of fabric away from my breasts and expose every inch of my skin to him, but he doesn't. Instead, he lowers himself on top of me and, with his eyes drifting shut, brushes his lips across mine, not in a kiss but something similar.

Butterflies don't even come close to describing the powerful flapping sensation in my belly as our breaths mix and I get my first taste of him.

I'm aroused to a level I have never experienced before, and the only thought in my head is that I want more. More of his hands on me and his words in my ear. More of the connection that hasn't stopped moving between us since I saw him on the beach.

With that thought burning in my mind, I thread my fingers through the soft hairs at the back of his head and pull him closer to me. He sucks in a sharp breath right before our lips fully meet.

It's electrifying, world flipping. Life changing.

The feeling of his lips on mine has my lungs seizing and heart thrashing. I gasp into his mouth, and he silences me by deepening the kiss and giving my tongue a gentle, teasing stroke with his.

Tyler moans his approval, and I shudder at the sound.

"I need to feel you," he rasps before I feel calloused fingers brushing my thighs.

I part them in approval. "Please."

His eyes flare as he sits back on his knees and pulls my bikini bottoms off, throwing them to the side. He grabs my knees and pushes them up, spreading me, exposing every inch of my wet pink flesh to him. I suck in a breath when his tongue darts out and wets his lips.

"*Fuck*. I knew you'd have a pretty pussy."

His approval lights me up like a fireworks show. I knew he would be like this—dirty-mouthed and confident. That's who he is. And it's exactly how I want him right now.

My eyes wander to the large bulge in his swim trunks, warmth filling my belly. "Your turn."

"Not yet."

A sound of protest escapes me before Tyler's sliding down the mattress and leaning between my legs. When he inhales deeply, I nearly combust.

With his lips spread in an arrogant smile, he slashes my pussy with his tongue, tasting me. He groans and presses deeper, exploring me in ways I only fantasized about in the dark of my bedroom.

"Tyler," I gasp when his lips wrap around my clit and suck. My hands fly to his head and grab at his hair with a savage ferocity. He nips at the swollen bud in punishment despite the guttural groan of pleasure I feel vibrate against my centre when I pull too hard.

"Don't rip it all out, baby. Let me keep some."

"Holy shit you have a dirty mouth," I whimper, lifting my hips in search of his tongue.

He reaches up with one hand and grabs my hip to push me into the mattress. His thumb brushes my hip bone, making me shudder. "And your pussy is just as greedy as it is pretty."

His breaths hit the burning skin between my legs as he hovers there, keeping his distance while watching me writhe with need beneath half-lidded eyes. Frustration blooms like a thorn-covered rose in my belly.

"Are you going to fuck me anytime soon, or should I go back to the beach and find another willing participant?" I hiss. When his eyes flare with something dark and daring, I pry my fingers from his hair and keep talking. "You may be out-of-this-world hot, Tyler, but I don't need someone as hot as you to scratch this itch. All I do need right now is a dick between my legs, and if you aren't up for the job—"

Tyler moves quickly, too quickly for me to prepare myself.

Suddenly, he's hovering over me. He grinds his pelvis against mine, and the feeling of his thick, hard cock pressing against my clit sends my head flying back. I gasp when his mouth finds my neck, his lips parted and wet against the hot skin.

He pulls back just enough to look me in the eyes. "The only cock you'll be feeling for the rest of this trip is this one, Gray. You'll feel it in here—" He slides a hand down my stomach and dips a finger inside of me. "—and here." His other hand leaves my hip, and his thumb draws a line up the centre of my throat.

My eyes go wide, and my lips part. I should be fighting him on this, telling him that the idea isn't at all appealing, but when I clench around the finger pumping inside of me, I know that option is no longer on the table. If it even was in the first place.

His smile is sinister as he slides another finger inside of my wetness. "Do you understand, Gracie?"

"What about after this trip?" I ask on a shuddered breath. Pleasure is a whirlpool in my belly. "What do we do then?"

Tyler curls his fingers, and I arch into him. My untied bikini top slips away, exposing my naked breasts. He drops his eyes to my chest and groans low in his throat. "We pretend this week never happened. I won't ever touch you like this again."

I shake my head. "No." Not happening.

"Yes."

He clenches his jaw and twists his fingers until he finds my G-spot. The sudden pleasure has my vision blurring and muscles tensing in preparation for a blinding climax. I chomp down on my tongue in an attempt to fight it but lose miserably when Tyler presses down on my clit with his thumb, rotating it over and over until I give in.

"Come for me, baby. Soak my fucking hand,"

I do. Holy shit do I ever. White-hot pleasure crashes into me harder than ever before as I come, crying out Tyler's name.

My pussy thumps with the aftershocks, but before I have a chance to collect myself, the broad head of Tyler's cock is nudging my entrance, covered in a condom I didn't notice him put on.

His board shorts are gone, leaving him completely naked. I'm no better than a horny dog as I stare at all of him for the very first time. At the strong curve of his hips, the hard bulging muscles in his thighs as he holds himself up, and the deep lines of his Adonis belt. I've seen him shirtless countless times just in the past couple of days alone, but looking at him now is a completely different experience. Now I know for certain that the line of short dark hairs beneath his belly button does continue all the way to the base of his cock and that the tattoo that only ever peaks above the waistband of his pants is indeed as gruesome as I imagined it would be.

An exposed bloody heart wrapped tight in chains is inked on his left hip. It's my first real look at what lies behind the steel walls of his soul, and before I know it, I'm reaching out to touch the design, my fingers gentle, cautious.

He flinches but lets me touch him, and I don't dare question him on it.

I take my time exploring the ink before sliding my nails across his groin and then further down, letting them scratch at the curls at the base of his erection.

"Gracie," he hisses. His hand covers mine, halting my movements. I lift an eyebrow. "You can show me how well you suck cock after I've been inside you, okay?"

Good Lord.

I nod and settle my hand on the dip in his waist instead, as if to give myself some control of what happens next. I learn quickly how naïve that thought was when his hips move, and the blunt tip of his cock brushes my entrance again, this time slipping inside, stretching me enough to invoke a slight flicker of pain. I gasp when he sinks deeper. He stills.

His voice is pained. "Are you okay?"

I wrap my arms around him and press the tips of my fingers into his back to gain leverage before twirling my hips and pushing myself further down his length. His eyes go wide before falling shut, pleasure tightening his features.

"Take that as a yes, then," he grunts once I've taken the entire length of him inside of me. Opening his eyes, he holds my stare as he slides out and rubs his tip over my clit before slowly pushing back in. "*Fuck* you feel good."

I whimper at the abrupt feeling of fullness that's taken over me but revel in it at the same time. It's satisfaction and pleasure stronger than I've ever felt, and when Tyler's thrusts grow harder and faster, I lose all inhibitions.

"Kiss me," I plead, looking into the dark pits of his eyes and growing more confident with each flicker of light I find. He falls to his elbows over me and brushes his mouth over mine. "Please."

Our mouths collide, Tyler's owning mine in a dominant kiss that only stokes the flames licking my insides. I moan against his lips when he lifts his hips and rubs my inner walls in the most addicting way.

He parts my lips with his tongue and reaches between our sweaty bodies to play with my clit. My toes curl as my climax builds and builds until it reaches its boiling point, bubbling over.

"Ty—" I cry before my climax steals my breath. My walls flutter around his shaft, and he shoves his face into my neck and exhales shakily.

He stops thrusting and growls, "Good girl, Gray. Good fucking girl," as he hits his own high.

It takes a few moments for us to catch our breath, and when we do, an awkward tension fills the air between us, the kind that makes you want to run and hide. Only I can't run and hide, not when I have a two-hundred-and-twenty-pound man hovering above me and jelly for leg muscles.

Tyler averts his eyes to the headboard above me as he pulls out and slides the condom off. He makes quick work of getting off the bed and disappearing into the bathroom, not sparing me a glance as he does.

I try not to let the panic I saw peeking through his calm façade hurt me, but I should know better than that by now. My feelings toward Tyler have been unreturned for so long now that although my head might know this didn't mean anything, my heart refuses to listen. To the stupid organ crying out for the guy who's hiding from me in the bathroom, what just happened between us was a love confession worthy of the big screen.

With a weighted sigh, I close my eyes and wait for him to finish in the bathroom, knowing damn well that I've lost him for now.

7

Oakley

I RAP MY KNUCKLES ON ADAM'S HOTEL ROOM DOOR AND wait.

There's loud shuffling from inside before the door is whipped open a second later. Adam is naked aside from a small towel tied around his waist. Not one to get shy, he doesn't seem at all bothered by his nakedness. He leans confidently in the doorway and stares at me.

Running his fingers through his wet hair, he says, "Morning, Lee. What can I do for you?"

A thickly accented voice calls out his name from inside the room, and I cock a brow. "You entertaining back there?"

He grins. "Mhm. It's a sold-out show, though, man. Better luck next time."

I snort a laugh. "My loss." The woman calls his name a second time, and I try to sneak a peek over his shoulder. Adam sidesteps me and shoves me back. "What's her name?"

"Now, why would I tell you that?"

"Right, so you don't know it, then."

"In my defense, we weren't really all about introductions last night," Adam rushes out. I laugh, and he continues. "How about we skip the rest of this conversation altogether so that I can get back to my guest."

He tries to shut the door in my face, but I stop it with my foot. "Not so fast. Ava sent me here to ask if you were up for a Sea-Doo ride today."

"She couldn't have texted me that?"

"She did. And FaceTimed you three times."

He looks over his shoulder as if in search of his phone before getting distracted. I immediately want to turn and leave when he lifts his fist to his mouth and groans.

"I was occupied," he mumbles.

I shake my head and laugh. "Clearly. I'll let Ava know that we will see you after."

He blinks, shaking himself out of his haze, and turns to me with an appreciative smile. "Thanks, Lee. I'll make it up to her tomorrow."

I give him a pointed stare. "You better. It won't be me that comes to ride your ass if you don't."

If there's anyone who can put Adam on his ass, it's Ava. She's one of the only people on this Earth he would do anything for. That once scared me, but now in a sense, it calms me. It's nice knowing there will always be someone besides me who will do anything to take care of her. I'm just happy that his protectiveness stems from friendship and not romantic feelings anymore.

I guarantee we wouldn't be standing here talking like best buddies if I thought the opposite.

"You have my word. Don't forget sunscreen, yeah?"

"As if. You know how Ava is about preparation. She had already gone through our beach bag twice before I left to track your ass down."

Adam smiles. "Good point."

"Adaaaaam," his female companion coos. "La cama se está enfriando."

I look at Adam expectantly. "What did she say?"

He shrugs. "No clue. But I'm going to go try and find out. Thanks for dropping by."

Rolling my eyes, I step back and let him close the door.

Gracie's room is only two doors down from Adam's, so I go there next. It's not unusual for my sister to sleep in to ungodly afternoon hours, or to just ignore texts, so I wasn't surprised when Ava told me she hadn't answered her either this morning.

Come to think of it, it's not a shock that none of our friends answered their phones this morning. Tyler is known to avoid human contact most days, and a vacation wouldn't change that. If anything, I think it's made his introvert ways even more prominent.

Selfishly, I would be relieved to get to spend the day on the ocean alone with Ava. We deserve it after how busy our lives have been. It's a miracle we could even wrangle this trip together between my preseason training, Ava's new job at the youth home, and her course load at school. Not to mention we're still living three hours apart.

I'm so desperate for her to finish school and move in with me that I have a calendar in my Seattle apartment with her graduation date circled over and over. It can't come soon enough.

I knock on Gracie's door and blow out a tight breath as I lean against the adjacent wall and wait. Scratching at my jaw, I fall back into my thoughts.

Ava's dream has always been to help children who are in the position she was for the majority of her youth, and we knew it wouldn't be easy, but I for one wasn't expecting a job at a youth home to be this hard on her. I should have known better.

She spends long days at the home with kids who have a nasty relationship with authority and a worse one with affection or even kindness in general. Regardless of the fact that I know it stems from poor childhood experiences and broken hearts, it's hard watching the toll it all has on her.

Every verbal attack she's the victim of or obvious flinch and whimper of a child only pushes on the sore parts of her heart.

I blink a few times to clear my head when my phone dings from the pocket of my shorts. After pulling it out, I look at the screen and frown.

Shit Disturber: *Just ran into Ava. If ur at my room, leave. I'm not there.*

Me: *Where are you?*

The bubbles pop up in the chat before disappearing. I'm about to double text when they appear again, and another text comes through.

Shit Disturber: *Out.*

Me: *Are you okay?*

Shit Disturber: *Ya dad. Enjoy ur day with Ava*

Huh. I'm not sure if I should be relieved or worried. No, she can take care of herself. As much as she loves to call me dad, I know I can be a tad overbearing at times. This is as much a vacation for her as it is for the rest of us. I have to trust that she'll make good decisions while we're here.

I open my conversation with Tyler only to find a message from him waiting for me, having come in at the same time as Gracie's.

Bateman: *Not leaving my room today. Have fun on the mini boats.*

There's a small prick of worry in my stomach. *Stop*. It's a coincidence.

Me: *Okay. See you at dinner?*

Bateman: *Just tell me when and where.*

Alright. I can always grill them both then. Gracie has never been a good liar; her nose crinkles every time she tries.

Slipping my phone back into my pocket, I head back in the direction of our room, more antsy than before to get to my girl.

AVA'S ARMS wrap tight around my middle as I press the gas on the Jet Ski and send us shooting through the ocean. The front end lifts when we hit a large wave, and she squeals in my ear.

"Oakley! If I fall off of this thing, I swear to Go—" She's silenced by a spray of water. I hear her gasp and burst out laughing.

Looking over my shoulder, I laugh even harder, to the point my stomach begins to ache. "A bit wet, sweetheart?"

"You're an asshole," she says, wiping her eyes. The mass of brown hair she had tied on the top of her head is sagging, heavy with ocean water.

I release the gas and reach behind me, grabbing her thigh and squeezing. Despite her annoyance, she scootches forward until our life jackets are squished together.

"Mean girl." My grin is big enough I'm sure they can see it back at the beach. "You want to drive this thing for a bit?"

Ava shakes her head, her lips brushing my neck, igniting a wave of electric shocks from the point of contact. I shiver, and she unlaces her hands from my middle and begins unzipping my life jacket. Once it's hanging open, she splays her hands on my chest, warm palms to wet abs.

"I'm good back here. As long as you don't soak me again."

"Are you sure? Getting you soaked is a favourite pastime of mine."

She snorts a laugh. "You've been spending too much time with Adam. His awful lines are rubbing off on you."

"No, baby. The only person rubbing on me right now is you."

"Okay, that one was pretty good," she replies, slightly breathless. I sneak a look at her over my shoulder and instantly notice how pink her cheeks are.

Looking forward again, I snicker, "Are you feeling warm? You look a little pink. Should I take us back to the beach?"

"No!" she rushes out. "I'm not feeling warm."

"Are you sure?"

Her nails scratch at my abs before slipping further down my

body and toying with the band of my swim trunks. My breath hitches when she presses an open-mouthed kiss to the back of my neck.

"Stop teasing me, Oakley Hutton, or you'll get as good as you give."

"That so?" I murmur.

The Jet Ski is nearly still, just coasting with the movement of the water. Silence welcomes us now that we're a far enough distance away from the beach and drifting closer to the small alcove I was heading for.

Ava hums low in her throat. "Yes. I wouldn't recommend testing me."

Of course, that only makes me want to test her that much more. "Is that reverse psychology, Ms. Layton?"

Her laugh paints my back. "It might be."

"In that case, why don't you let go of me so I can spin around and we can discuss this face to—fuuuck," I groan when the little minx drips her hand into my shorts and grabs my cock. She brushes her thumb over the tip, and I shudder.

"What was that?"

I squeeze my eyes shut and try to focus on not busting my load in my shorts with a single touch from Ava. My words are rough, barely scraped together as she starts to stroke me.

"Keep doing that and you're going to get fucked, sweetheart."

"Right here? Right now?"

"Yeah, Ava. Right here. Right. Now."

She gasps when I pull the keys out of the Jet Ski, clip them on my shorts, and spin around so quickly I have to grip her thighs to keep her from falling off. With my knees on either side of hers, I feel more in control of the moment.

"Fuck, you're gorgeous," I swear. She bats her lashes and smiles shyly. As if she has any reason to be shy. I've never seen a more beautiful woman, and I know I never will.

With light brown freckles splattered across her nose from spending so much time in the sun and lust-drunk green eyes that look brighter than usual, she's all mine. And I plan on keeping her.

Our eyes collide, and I feel the force behind the intense emotion in her stare deep in my chest. Like the weight of a thunder jacket, it's secure, strong, reassuring. Everything I needed, but nothing I was expecting. That's the best way to describe more than just how I feel, but the woman who *makes* me feel this way.

Ava blinks at me slowly before pushing the life jacket from my shoulders and replacing it with her hands. Using my shoulders as leverage to close the distance between us, she presses her soft pink lips to my rougher ones.

And just like that, I'm lost in her again.

8

Ava

OAKLEY KISSES ME BACK WITH A GENTLE ROUGHNESS.

He's a master of the art, a puppeteer using our mouths in the exact right way. My eyes drift shut as I hand over control, content with letting him be in charge now. His tongue swipes across the seam of my lips, asking for entrance, and I open without hesitation.

A rough noise escapes him, vibrating against my mouth when I press my fingers deeper into the strong, thick muscles of his shoulders. I lift my legs and drape them over his thighs before pulling my body even closer to his.

Our kiss breaks when he asks, "Do you want me to get us back to the resort?"

My answer is immediate. "No."

"No?"

A new feeling of bravery takes life inside of me, and I don't know if it's from the heat or the intensity sparking like a loose wire in water between us, but I don't want to lose it. So, I chase it.

Without thinking too much, I rotate my hips and brush my core against the straining bulge in his swim trunks.

"There's nobody around," I whisper.

His fingers curl around the back of my neck, and he pulls me close, our foreheads touching. With dark eyes twinkling with sin, he uses his other hand to grip my waist and pull me onto his lap.

"Are you sure? I can have us back in a few minutes."

"No. I want you now." I'm practically panting.

"Then I need this off of you." He pulls at the life jacket zipper and has the whole thing off and hanging from the Jet Ski handlebars before I realize what he's done.

My eyes roll back in pleasure when I feel him lift his hips and grind against my core. The layers between us are suddenly too much. My movements are frantic as I reach for the band of his shorts and pull at them.

"Ava," he chokes, placing a hand over mine. "Are you pos—"

I shush him. "Ask me if I'm sure again and I'll jump off this thing and swim back." I grab the hard length of him over his shorts and squeeze gently. "I need you right now."

He groans and releases my neck, reaching between us to glide a finger over my puffed lower lips. His eyes flare when he feels the slick material. "Then you'll get me."

In one swift movement, my bikini bottoms are pulled to the side and one long finger enters me. My breath catches on a moan.

"You're perfect. Everything about you," he breathes. His eyes hold mine as he slips a second finger inside and curls them with precision, rubbing them against my G-spot with an expertise that has me pulsing around his fingers.

"More," I gasp.

He nods frantically, and with the same urgency that I feel, removes his fingers and with an arm around my back, stands just enough to pull his shorts down and free his cock.

I swallow thickly and stare at the glistening tip. It doesn't matter how many times I see it, I'm always shocked that it fits inside of me.

"I'll never get tired of you staring at me like that."

I look up and find him smiling. "I could say the same thing."

He wraps his hand around himself and strokes a few times as I hold his shoulders and use his thighs as leverage and lift myself until I hover over him. His crown brushes my clit, and I whimper.

"Shit," he grunts, lining himself up with my opening. When he pushes inside and I start to lower myself down the length of him, he curses, "So tight. Like you were made for me."

I nod frantically through the bite of pain as he stretches me. As soon as I bottom out, my head falls back, the pain now mixing with ecstasy.

His arms wind around me and pull me close before I'm being lifted into the air, spun around, and placed down on my back, the leather seat warm against my back. Oakley releases me and grabs my thighs instead, dragging me toward where he's now standing on the back of the Jet Ski, his feet planted on the floorboards. My legs fall open when he presses down on my pelvis, pulls my bikini to the side again, and enters me in one thrust.

I cry out at the sudden fullness and let my head hit the seat, not able to keep it up. His fingers splay across the skin of my pelvis before cupping my hip, using the leverage to increase his thrusts.

The Jet Ski rocks on the water with every movement of Oakley's hips, creating our own waves.

Oakley groans low in his throat and uses his other hand to toy with my pussy, his fingers finding my clit and playing with it the way he knows will have me crying his name for the entire ocean to hear.

"That's it, baby. You're taking me so well," he praises me, voice tight with pleasure.

He thrusts hard and hits a place inside me that makes stars flood my vision. My back arches, and I cry out his name.

Oakley spins his finger around my clit, and my climax builds and builds until I'm struggling to fight it off. *Not yet.* I want to get there together.

I release a shaky breath of relief when his movements become frantic, and he says, "*Shit.* I'm going to come. Where do you want it, baby? Tell me to pull out, or I'm going to fill you up."

His words set me off. My muscles lock up as I come, my walls fluttering around his cock and squeezing him tight, refusing to let him pull away.

"Inside," I beg. There's no time to question where the hell the want to have his cum inside of me came from before he's bowing his back and cursing under his breath.

He slams into me for a final time, and warmth coats my insides as he climaxes.

"God, Ava," he says on a breath, gifting me a breathtaking smile.

I smile back. "I never expected you to have a breeding kink."

He eases himself out, and I wince at the raw feeling between my legs as my bikini bottoms fall back in place. The pain doesn't dim the after-sex bliss, though. If anything, it only makes it more real.

"Me? You weren't all that opposed to the idea either," he teases before mocking me, "Insiiide. Don't lose a drop!"

I roll my eyes. "I did not say all that, you drama queen."

"You didn't have to. You were squeezing me so tight I couldn't have pulled out even if I wanted to."

"Shut up." I swat his chest. He tugs up his swim trunks. "Do you have anything I can use to clean up? I wasn't expecting to get pounded on a Jet Ski when I got ready this morning."

His green eyes twinkle. "I don't know, I find it hot as hell to think of you riding back to the resort full of my cum. If you weren't on birth control, you would probably be pregnant already."

I snort a laugh and push myself into a sitting position. As the ocean breeze moves through my hair, I inwardly wince at how much of a mess I must look like right about now. My bun is loose and flops from side to side as I move my head. *Cute.*

"And my dad would kill you. He's adamant about us being married before having a baby."

The last time my father brought up his future grandchildren, he nearly blew a blood vessel in his face. Like any parent, he's both excited yet terrified for us to bring a small human being into the world. Mom, on the other hand, well, she's never been totally normal. If it were up to her, we would be on baby number two already.

"And what about you? What do you think?" he asks, suddenly serious.

I straighten my spine and watch him curiously. "You want to have this conversation now?"

He shrugs. "Why not? At least I have you trapped, so you can't run."

"I wouldn't run away even if we were on land."

His face morphs into a *really* expression.

"Whatever," I grumble. Maybe I would have found a way to avoid the conversation, but only because the idea of having a baby scares me. Really, who doesn't it scare?

Oakley sits on the set, facing me. "We've talked about the future countless times but somehow always avoid *really* talking about kids. As in whether or not they're something that could happen in the nearish future. Do you not want them?"

I shake my head. "I want them. I love kids."

"Then what is it? Because I don't know if I'm ready to be a dad, say, tomorrow, but I know it's something that I would like in the next couple of years. Obviously you're still in school, but you're graduating soon too."

I gather my fear and flick it away. It's Oakley—he won't judge me no matter what I say.

"I want to be a mom. I just don't know if I would be a good one. What if I turn out to be a complete failure? What if our kids grow up to hate me?" *What if you don't love me as much after there's someone else in the picture?*

He reaches toward me and gathers my hands in his. There's so much love in his eyes it steals my breath.

"You're going to make a phenomenal mother, Octavia. Not only are you the most outrageously kind person I've ever met, but you love so deeply that our kids won't ever doubt for a second that you aren't completely obsessed with them. They won't spend a day wondering if they're cared for. Your childhood doesn't define you, baby. If anything, it showed you the kind of mother you don't want to be. You're Lily's daughter, and she didn't raise you to fear your future."

Tears swell in my eyes by the time he's done speaking. I suck in a shaky breath and nod once, squeezing his hands.

"I don't know how I got lucky enough to have you in my life," I admit.

He releases my hands and cups my face before swiping away my tears with two large thumbs. "I ask myself the same question every single day."

"I would love to have babies with you, Oakley Hutton. And whenever you decide is the right time, I want to marry you. I want you to be my husband."

He grins. "Soon, my love. I promise."

I've never been a patient person, or at least not when it comes to things that I'm desperate to have, but when it comes to this, I've been trying. Even if I do find myself searching through Oakley's dresser drawers in search of a ring box once a month.

"You brought up marrying me a year ago now. I'm getting antsy."

He leans in and kisses my nose. "I know, and I plan on making you Mrs. Octavia Hutton as soon as possible. The timing has to be perfect, and with you snooping through my drawers all the time, who knows when that might be."

My eyes go wide. "You know?"

"Of course I know. I just love you enough not to have said anything to spoil your fun."

I laugh loudly, my head falling back. This man . . . he's special. I've known it since the first moment I laid eyes on him, and I'll remember it for the rest of my life.

9

Tyler

I RELEASE GRACIE'S HAIR, AND SHE SPUTTERS OFF MY dick with a greedy inhale.

Her lips are swollen, and spit drips from the corners of her mouth, but fuck, she's gorgeous. I scrape my nails against her scalp and groan at the needy sound that escapes her before she's being silenced with my cock again.

"Who the fuck taught you to suck dick, Gracie," I rumble when she swirls her tongue around the tip and over the slit that I know is leaking precum like a motherfucker.

She hums, watching me coyly beneath her lashes. The vibrations act like shocks of electricity in my veins. I use the hair wrapped around my fist to pull her back, a new possessiveness clouding my judgment.

"Who?" I ask tightly.

She smiles. "Why? Don't tell me you want to thank him."

"It was that fucker Jim, wasn't it?"

"Jacob," she corrects me with a giggle. Her fist tightens around my length and pumps at a slow, teasing pace. "And what if it was? Why does it matter who taught me what I know?"

Why? Maybe because the thought of her with anyone else's dick in her mouth has my insides churning in a bitter rage, and that is fucked up on so many levels. "I want to give them props," I lie.

She rolls her eyes. "Right. Well, I'll make sure to let Jacob know you approve of his lessons, then."

I scowl and release her hair. She blinks at me curiously. "Move up and sit on my face, then put my dick in your mouth again before the thought of that dweeb makes me soft."

"Oh," she breathes, nodding.

"The only O I want to hear is the one that will come after I have my tongue in your pussy, Gracie."

Her pupils dilate before she's moving to give me space to lie back on the bed and then crawling up my body. I grip her thighs when they move to bracket my head and tilt my chin to flick her pussy with my tongue. "Sit," I order.

"Shit," she hisses when I pull her down and cover her slit with my mouth. Her taste explodes on my tongue, and my cock twitches.

"Put my cock in your mouth, baby," I mumble against her.

She's leaking like a fucking faucet, and I can't get enough. Swirling my tongue around her opening, I dig my fingers into the hard muscles of her thighs and pull her even further back.

"Tyler," she gasps, grabbing me in her hand and hovering her mouth over the head. "Can you still breathe?"

My laugh hits her clit, and she jolts. "Let me suffocate, sweetheart. I want to meet the devil with the taste of your pussy on my tongue."

The words have barely escaped when she swallows my cock, taking it deeper and deeper until it hits the back of her throat. My thighs clench as I keep myself from moving and pushing her to take it even further.

I find her clit with my tongue and suck it into my mouth before softly nipping at it. Soothing the sting, I lap at her and moan at the feel of her silky-smooth skin.

"Jesus fuck," I curse when she swallows around me. The telltale sensation of an orgasm has me moving. Before she has the chance to do anything but squeal in surprise, I have her on her stomach on the bed, legs spread wide for me. "Lift your hips."

She flips her hair over her shoulder and looks back at me, doing exactly as I ordered.

I sit on my knees behind her and cup her ass in both hands, testing the weight of it in my palms. She pushes back into my grip, mischief in her eyes.

"Well? Do I pass inspection?"

"With flying colours."

She hums and snakes a hand beneath her body, slipping it between her legs and spreading herself open for me. "I think you missed a spot."

I can't stop my eyes from widening in surprise at her boldness. Every time I think she can't surprise me more, she goes and damn well does.

My words are rough, pained. "We can't have that."

Sliding my hand from her ass, I move it between her legs and slip a finger inside of her with ease, feeling the tight grip of her inner walls around it.

"I was thinking you could use something a bit bigger," she rasps, wiggling her hips.

"That so?"

I push another two fingers inside. "Like that?"

She shakes her head. "Bigger."

Fisting my cock, I stroke it slowly, utterly entranced by the want in her eyes as she watches me. Having someone look at you the way Gracie looks at me would excite anyone. But it does far more than just excite me. It tempts me to actually do something about it. And that's not something I can afford to think about.

I tighten my fist and watch a bead of precum leak from the tip before collecting it with the pad of my thumb and releasing my cock. Gracie must realize what I plan on doing because she parts her lips and sticks her tongue out.

"Good girl," I grunt. Reaching around her, I slide my thumb

into her mouth and swallow hard when she sucks it clean. "That's the only taste you get."

"I won't be getting anything until you stop talking and fuck me."

I laugh lowly while wrapping an arm around her waist and hoisting her up. She reaches for me when I start to sink inside of her, whimpering once I bottom out.

"How's that?" I pull out and grab her hips, slamming her back as I thrust back in.

"Good. So good," she pants. Her head falls forward, her hair acting as a veil around her face. "I'm close already. Shit, like really close."

With a newfound vigor, I pick up speed, hissing in pleasure as it spikes. The headboard slams into the wall, and I get an idea.

"Grab the headboard."

She does, and I take advantage of the new angle, using it to hit the spot inside of her that hasn't failed to set her off so far. At the same time, I move my hand between her legs and twirl my finger around her clit. She bucks against me, her grip on the headboard so tight her knuckles are white.

I bite back my growl when her sex starts to flutter around me, her walls contracting and squeezing me tight.

"That's it, Gracie. Let me have it."

Her head rears back as she comes. "Tyler," she cries, the sound music to my ears.

My balls tighten, and as soon as she goes lax, I pull out and replace her pussy with my fist, stroking myself until I'm spraying thick ropes of cum on her lower back. Grunting, I splay my hand over it and smear it into her skin. It's a caveman act. Something you do to mark your territory, and for some reason, that only encourages me.

I'm dragging it over her ass cheeks like fucking lotion when she looks at me over her shoulder and with deep pink cheeks asks, "What are you doing?"

"I don't know," I admit gruffly.

Gracie pushes back, and I'm forced to remove my hand when her back hits my chest. My heart lurches, beating hard and fast as she relaxes against me and loops an arm around my neck.

"Well, I liked it," she whispers.

I freeze. Four words and the walls start to close in. Four simple, harmless words lacking anything but mild appreciation, and I'm clearing my throat and easing away from her.

"I need to wash my hands."

She drops her hands to the mattress and flips onto her back. Her glare is nearly sharp enough to cut down the steel walls around me. *Nearly.*

"One of these days, your immediate regret every time we have sex is going to affect my mental health. You should work on not making it so obvious."

I divert my eyes to the bathroom door. "It's not regret."

"No? Because it looks like it to me. This is the exact same thing you did yesterday before running off and not speaking to me until this morning."

"Fuck, Gracie. I don't even know what I'm doing here. We both just lied to your brother about not wanting to go out with them, and for what? Nothing is going to come from this."

She flinches, hurt swimming in her eyes. I swallow my guilt.

"If you don't know why you're here with me, then leave. Right now." Her voice is cold, emotionless. It strikes me harder than a brick to the head.

"Graci—"

"Go!" she shouts, angrier than I've ever seen her. "Go wash your fucking hands of this, and then get out of my room."

I nod. There's nothing I can say right now that she wants to hear. I know I don't like to see her upset, but that doesn't change anything.

I'm not the white knight.

I'm the villain that would end up trapping her in a steel tower and refuse to let her back down. She would suffocate in my world. Gracie Hutton is too bright to spend her life in my darkness.

It's silent as I get off the bed and head to the bathroom. It's painful to try to pretend like I'm not single-handedly crumbling a human heart in my hands as I do.

I catch movement from the corner of my eye and turn to see her on her side, facing the wall on the opposite side of the room. My cum is dried to her skin, and I hate myself a little bit more for that.

With a shake of my head, I walk into the bathroom and wet a washcloth with warm water before going back to the bed. Gracie flinches when I start wiping her back but doesn't say anything. I might be an absolute asshole, but I'm not a Neanderthal. She deserves whatever mildly soft part of me I can give her.

The silence is heavy as I move the cloth between her legs and then back up before heading for the bathroom again. This time when I get away, I shut the door and slam my head against it.

What the fuck am I going to do now?

10

Adam

Ava spots me heading toward their table in the fancy Italian restaurant they chose for dinner and shouts, "Look who decided to leave his sex dungeon!"

I pull at the collar of my button-up shirt and flash her a grin. It's hotter than Satan's asshole in Mexico right now, and if I had it my way, I wouldn't have to wear a shirt for the duration of our stay. But alas, *no shoes, no shirt, no service*, and I'm starving.

Tyler, Gracie, Oakley, and Ava are seated at a table that looks out at the ocean, an array of candles lit in the centre. The white tablecloth drapes over the sides of the table and brushes their knees.

"I couldn't deny my hunger any longer, O baby," I shoot back.

Tyler rolls his eyes and brings his glass of brown—my guess, whiskey—to his mouth while Gracie eyes mine with obvious curiosity.

"Where's your friend?" she asks when I pull out the empty chair between her and Oakley and sit.

"Were you hoping to make a new friend?" I counter.

"Not really. But you know me, a curious Claudia."

I snort a laugh. "I think it's a curious cat, Gray."

She bumps my shoulder. "Who cares. You obviously knew what I meant. Now tell me, are you going to see her again while we're here?"

Oakley sputters, "Doubt it."

"What does that mean?" I gasp.

"It means you didn't even know her name this morning," Ava cuts in with a sympathetic smile. "But you know Gray, she's—"

"A romantic," Tyler grumbles.

Gracie spins around in her chair until her eyes cut like daggers into the side of Tyler's head. "And? There's nothing wrong with wanting some romance. Not everyone can be an empty shell of a person who fears emotion."

Someone's breath hitches across the table while I lean my elbows on the table, settling in for a good show. It's been a long time coming since this fight broke out, and I for one can't wait.

I love my guy Tyler, but he's been poking at the wrong bear for too long. Gracie Hutton isn't one to take shit from anyone, not even the guy she's been obvious about crushing on. And boy has he *ever* been poking her. I'm almost certain he enjoys having her attention; he just won't ever admit it.

Tyler's eyes narrow to slits. "Romance is for the naïve. You're a perfect example of that."

"Has the waitress been around?" I ask and snatch the menu in front of Gracie. "My stomach is grumbling nonstop."

"Tyler," Oakley says, his voice thick with warning. "Watch it."

Gracie doesn't so much as flinch. She's far too angry for his insults to truly sink in. I'm sure it'll hit hard once they do, though.

"I may be naïve, but at least I'm not a walking cliché. The whole emotionally unavailable fuckboy is quite overdone, don't you think?" she spits.

"Apparently not. It hasn't stopped you from chasing at my heels."

I wince, and Gracie sucks in a sharp breath. Ava chooses the break in their arguing to say, "Okay, I think the point has gotten across, guys."

When I look away from a red-faced Gracie and toward Ava and Oakley, I gulp at the raging anger on Oakley's face. If he clenches his jaw any tighter, we might be spending the remainder of our night in the hospital. Ava rubs his shoulder in an effort to calm him down.

I rack my brain for something to say to extinguish the blaze, but Oakley beats me to it.

"Tyler. Come with me. Now," he growls before shoving away from the table and stalking off.

Silently, Tyler gets up and follows. I look at Ava. "Should I go too?"

"Please," she breathes.

I squeeze Gracie's shoulder, but she doesn't look at me. She's staring at the placemat on the table in front of her, blinking profusely. A small sniffle escapes her, and my heart constricts at seeing her so upset.

"Go, Adam," Ava urges when I don't make an effort to get up and follow the other two. I meet her sad eyes with a look of concern. "I've got her."

Still, my body refuses to move.

"I'm okay, Adam. Go make sure my brother doesn't end up in jail," Gracie croaks.

"Are you sure? I don't mind hanging out here. We could go get drunk and fall asleep on the beach if you wanted? I'm a super-fun drunk, I swear."

Ava laughs softly. "He's not lying. He also becomes quite funny with a bit of liquor in that rich-boy blood."

"What do you mean 'become'? I'm funny all the time," I protest.

"The number of lame sex jokes you've taught Oakley says otherwise."

"Nah, you love them. It gives him some layers. Like an ogre."

Gracie chokes on a laugh. "A Shrek fan, Adam?"

I grin. "Is the sky blue?"

"Actually, no. It's not," Ava answers smugly.

"You know, sometimes it's just nice to let someone think they know what they're talking about, O. Where's the generosity?"

She rolls her eyes. "Must have left it at home."

I hum and look at Gracie, relieved to see some of the sadness gone from her eyes. It's enough reassurance for me to feel okay about going to check on the misfits.

Pushing away from the table, I meet Ava's stare and nod.

"Give me a second, ladies. I'll be right back."

Gracie makes a sound of agreement before I'm walking away from the table and through the restaurant, toward the hallway where I saw the two guys disappear.

The telltale sound of hushed, angry voices confirms I'm on the right trail. With the lighting so dim, it's hard to make out the two large bodies standing far too close at the end of the hallway, which is a very good thing.

We don't need to go getting ourselves kicked out. I'm far too hungry.

"You need to deal with whatever it is that you're dealing with in your life, Tyler. But if you take out your frustrations on my sister like that again, I'll crush your windpipe and make you choke on the pieces." Oakley's words are nothing short of a promise.

"Noted," Tyler grumbles.

Oakley continues. "I know it's probably weird for you to be around her, knowing she likes you, but we gave you the opportunity to stay home. We didn't want you to have to spend a week feeling uncomfortable, but you insisted it would be okay."

That's news to me. I sink into the shadows and listen, content with eavesdropping for now.

"It *is* okay. Fuck. I know I shouldn't have gone at her like that back there. I feel like a goddamn dick already," Tyler says.

"It's good to know you can feel guilt after all, but it's not me you need to be telling this to."

A pause before Tyler releases a tight breath. "She won't want to talk to me."

Frustration is a prick in my side. He's completely oblivious when it comes to the inner workings of a woman. With my arms crossed, I step out of the shadows and say, "I beg to differ. I think you're the only one she wants to talk to right now."

Both men spin in the direction of my voice and move out of the shadows, side by side. My eyebrows lift when they slither into view, and I notice the red mark on Tyler's jaw.

I look at Oakley. "I was too late, it seems. Ava is going to have my balls for this."

"He punches like a kid," Tyler says, reaching up to brush his knuckles against the redness. He flinches, and I laugh.

"Do you want a redo?" Oakley asks.

"Pass."

"I bet you both a hundred bucks that out of the three of us, I have the hardest punch." I smirk. They both laugh.

"And how do you suggest we test this claim?" Oakley asks.

"Well, you and I could each punch Tyler, and then Tyler could punch you," I offer.

Tyler scoffs. "What the fuck kind of suggestion is that?"

"It's only fitting after the both of you ruined dinner."

"Me? What did I do?" Oakley guffaws. I smile.

"What's Gracie's punishment, then?" Tyler places his hands firmly on his hips. "She was giving it back just as good as I was."

I shrug. "Nothing. And you're older, so you should know better."

"She's eighteen, not twelve. No deal," he replies.

High heels click on the tile behind me, capturing our attention. I spin around to see Ava standing at the end of the hall with her hands on her hips.

"Are you done yet? The buffet is going to be out of the good stuff unless you hurry," she says.

Oakley breaks away from us and walks to his girl, collecting her in his arms. She giggles into his chest, and I find myself smiling at the happy sound.

I didn't think it was possible to be this happy for another person, but shit, it is. The smile on Ava's face every single time she sees Oakley would be enough to fix the most broken heart.

It took a few hard months to understand that she wasn't my person—not romantically, at least—but once I did, our friendship only got stronger, more impenetrable.

Thinking back on it now, I wouldn't change a single thing about our past. The good, bad, and ugly. Everything happens for a reason, and that has never felt truer than with us.

11

Oakley

After the . . . incident in the restaurant last night, a guys-only zip-lining adventure seemed like the only right thing to do.

Things are still a bit tense between Tyler and me, but hopefully with a little fresh air to clear our heads, we can work our shit out and move on. I'm not the type of guy to hold on to grudges, and I don't think Tyler is either, so this should be easy enough.

If not, well, I have no idea what to do next.

The three of us step off the shuttle bus, and Adam jogs ahead with the excitement of a child going through the Disneyland gates for the first time. I chuckle, and Tyler shakes his head.

"I've been wanting to go zip-lining since I was a kid," Adam says in awe. His eyes are wide, full of adventure as he looks around the rows of ATVs lined up beside a small log building.

None of us have been zip-lining before, and it's almost heartwarming to think that we'll all be experiencing it for the first time together.

Ava was the one who reserved our spots for today, having been the only one who has any experience with zip-lining. She was positive that we'll love it, and I don't doubt it. We all have a thrill for adrenaline, and what better way to feed that thrill than by soaring over treetops?

"You're telling me you never took your dad's black card and went on a zip-lining expedition before?" Tyler asks, seemingly unconvinced.

"Who the hell would I have gone with? Our personal chef?"

"I don't know, maybe your friends?" Tyler scoffs.

Adam gasps. "Wow. You're a bloody genius, Tyler Bateman. Why didn't I ever think of that?"

Tyler scowls. "Okay, jackass."

"I never had friends that wanted to do that kind of shit before, and even if I did, I never had the time after hockey started to become more of a priority for me."

I nod. "Fair enough. But at least we can do it now."

Adam grins at me before our attention is pulled to a man and a woman as they step out of the building, clipboards in hand.

The man looks to be a few years older than us, with a warm smile and sea-blue eyes. He exudes a calmness that I'm sure you would need when it comes to working with people who might start freaking out once it comes time to actually zip-line.

Gracie would be that person. When she was thirteen, our mom took us to an amusement park, and after convincing both of us that she could handle being thrown into the air on one of the more adrenaline-inducing rides, she ended up having a complete breakdown as soon as she was strapped into her seat.

She hasn't been to an amusement park since.

Tyler's shoulder bumps mine. "How many people do you think will chicken out when we get up there?"

"Two."

Adam sidles up on my other side, bouncing in place. "I'm going to be optimistic and say none."

"Maybe it will be you," Tyler says.

"As if. Maybe *you'll* get cold feet, Mr. I'm-not-afraid-of-anything," Adam retorts.

I snicker. "Let's hope neither of you back out. If you don't follow after me, I'm leaving without you."

Someone clears their throat, and the group turns to face the speaker. The older man I noticed earlier looks around the group and says, "Hello, everyone. I'm Miguel, and this is Isabella." He gestures to the woman beside him, and she gives us a wave. "We will be your guides for today. Please follow us inside to grab the ATV keys and a helmet. If you are riding with someone else, just grab a helmet. You've already been checked in on the shuttle, so once everyone is ready, we will head to the zip-line location."

There's a collective sound of agreement before we're all heading for the building behind our guides. We collect our helmets and keys quickly and make it back outside in record time. Adam jumps on an ATV at the very front of the pack, with Tyler and me grabbing the next two.

I insert the key and turn on my ATV, the rumble vibrating through my legs and up my spine. Grabbing the handlebars, I squeeze and let a smile part my lips.

"You look like a kid in a candy store," Tyler shouts at me. He's turned to face me, looking like he's gripping the handlebars of his ATV just as tight as I am.

I watch as the rest of our group gets settled on their ATVs and yell back, "I love quad rides. I haven't been on one in years, though." Not since I went out with my peewee team to our coach's empty farmland and ripped around on one of his ATVs. I'm still not over the impressive collection he had.

Adam swings around on his seat to face us. "How long of a ride is it again?"

"Twenty minutes, I think," I reply.

Just then, Miguel and Isabella step outside. It's Isabella who speaks this time, her Mexican roots thick in her accent.

"If everyone is ready, let us go!"

My eyes wander to Adam as he whoops loudly. I shake my head and a couple of minutes later follow behind Tyler up the trails in the wildlife, not forgetting to soak up every moment.

TYLER DRIFTS his ATV in a giant puddle and flings mud at me. It sticks to my arms and legs, narrowly missing my face.

His laugh is evil as he takes off, and I make a promise to myself to serve him a thick slice of payback pie on the way back.

Adam is already parked in the small clearing when Tyler and I get there. He yanks off his red helmet and slips it on the handlebars of his quad before getting off and stretching out his legs.

Once I'm pulling up beside him and turning off my ATV, I move to stand beside him and Tyler. The rest of the group is still trickling into the clearing when I turn to the guys and ask, "Do you know what the girls are doing today? Ava wouldn't tell me before I left the room this morning."

Tyler shakes his head. "No."

"I think Ava mentioned something about wanting to have a spa day before we went home, so that could be it," Adam says.

"Would make sense." I nod before curiosity nips at me. "Hey, do you wear clothes when getting a massage?"

"Can't say I've ever had a massage," Tyler grunts.

Adam only laughs at me. "I have a couple times. And I'm sure they're both covered with something."

"What does that mean? *Covered with something*?" I snap.

He laughs harder. "It means that I think they'll have a towel or something covering their asses. So no, neither your girlfriend nor sister is completely naked in the room."

"A towel? That's it?" Tyler asks, suddenly interested. I narrow my eyes on him.

"They probably kept their underwear on." Adam shrugs. His eyes bounce between the two of us with an odd fascination.

"And their bras?" I ask in a rush. This seems like a fucking nightmare. What kind of massage is this? My stomach tightens.

"Their tits are out?" Tyler growls. He turns to me, his face red. "We have to go back."

I double blink, taken aback by the sudden protectiveness. Is it for Ava or Gracie? Actually, neither seem like a better option when I think about it.

"Why do you care? And for God's sake, can you not say the word tits when in reference to my little sister?" My nose crinkles.

He releases a tight breath. "You're okay with them being naked, alone with some masseuse? Do we know if it's a guy?"

Adam snickers. "Could be."

"You're so not helping," I snap at him.

He rolls his eyes. "You know, this is probably why Ava didn't tell you what they were doing today. She knew you would go over-protective alpha male on her."

"That's *exactly* why she didn't tell us," Tyler mumbles.

I tighten my grip on the ATV key. "And why we need to go back and make sure no random man is seeing my girl's naked back, let alone the shape of her bare ass beneath a towel."

Adam moves quick, swiping the keys from my hand before doing the same to Tyler's. "No. You're staying here with me and getting a goddamn harness on."

Tyler tries to grab his key back, but with a shit-eating grin, Adam holds it above the band of his shorts. "Try me, Tyler Bateman, and these keys will go swimming in my balls."

"You're fucking gross," Tyler growls but relents.

I run a hand over my head and frown. "I don't like it."

"Well, I can guarantee that neither Ava or Gracie will enjoy you storming in like bats out of hell all because you were being jealous pricks," Adam says.

"I'm not jealous, asshole," Tyler is quick to blurt out. I want to believe him, but there's a small, relentless prick of doubt in my side that just won't go away. It's been there since yesterday morning.

I give my head a shake. "Let's just drop it. It looks like everyone's here now anyway."

Miguel is standing beside a small trail in the thick bush, his eyes on the clipboard in his hands. The air is muggy, and the bugs are out in full force, buzzing around and tickling my skin. Somehow, though, I don't mind.

Isabella waves a hand in the air. "If everyone is ready, follow us. Watch out for rocks in the trail."

"The last one to get there has to go down the zip-line first. We'll call you a test subject," Miguel jokes, eyes bright. At least, I think it's a joke.

A collective laugh rings out as everyone gathers their stuff, and we head toward the trail.

12

Adam

Adrenaline zips in my veins and trots in my stomach. I'm a live wire as my feet touch the ground, and I stumble slightly, trying to regain my balance.

With wobbly legs, I grab the top of my harness and grin. I take my helmet off and run a hand through my matted curls. "Holy shit that's fun."

Oakley nods from his spot beside a waist-high, triangular rock. His cheeks are pink, either from the wind or the heat of the sun. If it's the latter, Ava is going to lose her mind, considering she made him swear to slather himself in sunscreen before we got harnessed up and he didn't.

"The wind's picked up, right? That isn't just me?" he asks, looking up at the sky. He went down first, and the air was still at the time.

A large gust of warm wind knocks into us, blowing through my hair. "Nope. It's definitely picked up."

It's after the next burst of wind that we hear Tyler cry out in alarm. Oakley swivels in my direction, eyes wide.

"You heard that too, right?" he asks.

I nod. "Yeah." With quick steps, I head for the break in the trees the zip-line runs through. Craning my neck, I see a large figure stalled on the line, arms and legs flailing.

"What the fuck! Someone get me the fucking fuck off of here, or I swear to God—"

"No way," Oakley chokes. He bends forward and starts to laugh, the sound echoing around us. "There's . . . no way. This . . . this is . . . gold," he wheezes.

I unzip the pocket in my shorts and pull out my phone, swiping at the screen to open the camera. Turning on a video, I point the camera at Tyler and zoom in.

If I didn't know better, I would think that he looked a bit green, but he's too far away to be certain. What I do know for sure is that he's currently waving at the ground like a madman, as if either myself or Oakley will be able to climb up the zip-line and drag his ass down to the ground.

"This is the most beautiful karma," Oakley says once he's collected himself. He wipes his eyes with the back of his hand.

"Why do you think I'm recording this? I'm sending it to the group chat. Gracie will love it."

I zoom in to Tyler's dangling body as far as I can before the picture gets too blurry and catch him throwing up his middle finger. "He knows I'm recording," I snicker.

"Good."

I lift my hand and wave at him before turning off the recording. "He's definitely planning how he's going to kill us and where he'll hide our bodies."

Oakley laughs. "I'm pretty sure he planned my murder last night."

"How are things going since last night? I thought I was going to have to break up a brawl after you left the table at the restaurant."

Call me nosy, I don't care. Their drama is my drama, and I've never been a fan of that nasty bitch.

"I think it's okay. Today helped."

I hum. "Have you guys talked about it?"

Oakley looks at me, brows lifted. "What are you, our couple's counsellor?"

"If that's what you need me to be."

"We haven't talked about it. There hasn't really been time. But I'm not sure there's really anything to talk about. We usually just move past things like this." He sounds unsure, nervous.

"But this time is different?"

He looks at me with a seriousness in his eyes that surprises me. "You don't think there's anything going on with him and Gray, do you?"

My breath stutters. *Damn.* What the hell is the right answer here?

Do I think Tyler may have some sort of attraction to Gracie? Yes. Do I think he's into her the way she's into him? No way in hell. And I don't say that because she's not lovable—she's probably the most loveable person in the world—but because she's Gracie, and Tyler is so *very* much Tyler.

There isn't much I think could happen between them, but as much as I love Tyler, I think that what *could* possibly happen between them, albeit a small, small chance, would be exactly what Oakley is concerned about.

"I don't think he has feelings for her, if that's what you're asking me," I finally say.

He exhales and nods a few times. I feel nearly as relieved by his easy acceptance as he looks by my answer.

"Okay. Yeah, you're right. I guess I was just confused by his reaction to the spa talk earlier. He's never been like that before."

"Like what? Concerned?" I laugh.

He shakes his head. "No. I thought he looked . . . I don't know. Possessive? Jealous? But I was clearly in my own head about it."

I should tell him that I thought the same, but even with that strange attitude from Tyler, it doesn't change that I don't see them being romantically involved. Even being sexually involved is a stretch without more to go off.

"Maybe he's warming up to her. Wants to look out for her, you know?"

He doesn't appear to believe me but nods anyway. My guess is that he doesn't want to worry himself over what could be nothing. He's too smart.

"Well, should I send this video to the girls?" I ask, changing the subject.

That makes him smile. "Hell yeah."

I open the group chat and press Send.

Gracie

ANOTHER MOAN ESCAPES me as the woman doing my pedicure pushes her thumbs into my heel, working out the tension there. "God yes."

Ava sighs out in the chair beside me. "This must be what it feels like to take magic mushrooms."

I snort. "Magic mushrooms? Is that as wild as you'd ever get?"

"What do you mean? Is that not wild?"

"Oh, honey. You're so cute."

"Don't mock me, Gray. Don't forget I'm older than you," she warns.

I meet her playfully narrowed eyes with my innocently round ones. "I'm shaking in fear."

"You and your brother are so similar it's almost scary," she notes.

"Yeah, I've heard that once or twice." But only when it comes to our personalities. Looks-wise, we couldn't be any more different.

"What colour are you getting?" she asks, wiggling her toes. There's a bottle of sunflower-yellow polish on the floor beside the woman massaging her calves.

"Hot pink."

"No surprise there." She laughs.

I grin. "You know me. Always easy to please."

Her eyes go wide before returning to their normal size. "You're funny."

"Oh whatever. I *can* be easy to please. Better?"

It's not my fault that I have high standards. I was born that way. There's no point in trying to change myself eighteen years down the line. *If it's not broke, don't fix it.*

Ava is shaking her head, smiling to herself, when our phones ding. We both reach for them, but it's me that breaks the silence with a snorted laugh.

"This should be good," I say, unlocking the screen. Adam's message opens in our group chat.

Adam: *This one is for you Gray. Enjoy xoxoxoxo*

"Oh, my God," Ava gasps.

There's a video beneath the message with a photo of a zip-line, and I turn the volume up on my phone before pressing Play.

I raise a hand to my mouth and choke on a laugh when I see Tyler hanging from the zipline, flailing around like a baby bird trying to fly. He's shouting something, but the recording doesn't pick up what. My brother's laughter is loud in my phone's speakers.

"Is that Tyler?" Ava asks.

"That's Tyler," I confirm. I would recognize him anywhere.

The recording shakes, like Adam lost his balance or something, before Tyler's flipping him the bird and Adam's hand appears in the video. Oh boy, he's waving at him.

The video ends shortly after that, and with a stupid grin on my face, I type a message for the chat.

Me: *You'll pay 4 that l8er Adam. But know I loved it. Thank u*

Adam: *You're welcome. They're bringing him down right now*

Big bro <3: *His punishment will come soon I'm sure. You girls better fill a tub with ice. Adam will need it tonight.*

Ava: *No he won't. You won't let anything happen.*

Ava: *Right?*

Big bro <3: *Scouts honour*

Big bro <3: *Now tell me you wore underwear for your massage*

I sputter a laugh, turning to Ava. "He knew we were getting massages?"

She shakes her head rapidly. "No!" Realization dawns on her. "Adam. That sneaky shit."

Ava: *ADAM! *Angry face emoji**

Adam: *... he tortured it out of me.*

Big bro <3: *Liar. He gave up the information without a single threat. Might want to reconsider his best friend status, babe.*

Adam: *If you want me to yourself Lee, just say that. There's no need to play games*

Me: *Awe, when's the wedding?*

Tyler: *NEVER. They're both dead.*

Me: *Leave them alone. Ur lucky I wasn't there. I would have made sure they kept u up on that line until tomorrow morning*

Tyler: *And I would have found a way to tie you up there with me. Maybe upside down*

Adam: *Children, come on. There's no need for violence*

Ava: *Oakley? Did he get you?*

Big bro <3: *No. But we're getting ready to head back now. Talk soon. I love you both*

Me: *Leave Tyler there. Love u big bro*

Ava: *See you soon. *kissy face emoji* *red heart emoji**

"Some days they drive me crazy, and other days I can't believe I got so lucky," Ava sighs, tucking her phone away.

I put mine away and nod. There's a heavy feeling of hurt still in my chest after everything that has happened with Tyler over the past five days, but right now, it dims the slightest bit. "Yeah. Me either."

13

Tyler

MY FIST CONNECTS WITH GRACIE'S DOOR TWICE before it falls to my side. She's going to tell me to get fucked. That's what I would do if I were her. But it's too late to turn back now.

Soft footsteps sound behind the door before they stop. My chest constricts when the door still doesn't open a few moments later.

I sigh. "Open up, Gray. I know you're looking at me through the peephole."

A loud huff. "What are you doing here?"

"Open the door first. I want to talk."

"Okay, well, I don't."

The menace in her words doesn't surprise me. I'd say it's completely warranted. I should have been *here* yesterday, not zip-lining with my friends. Fuck, all yesterday did was allow me a space away from Gracie to feel even guiltier about what happened both inside of her room and afterward at dinner.

The odds of her forgiving me now, after I let her marinate in her hurt feelings for an entire day, are slim to none. But that doesn't mean that I won't at least try. She might not be my girl, but she's still family. I would have wound up in jail had any other prick hurt her the way I did.

I swallow my pride. "Please, Gray. Open the door."

Two beats later, she does.

It's a struggle not to show the effect she has on me, looking like a goddamn angel without trying.

Her hair is loose, cascading down her back in waves and shining under the early morning light that's slipping in beneath the window coverings. She blinks at me sleepily, and I have to divert my eyes before I end up falling to my knees in front of her and begging for forgiveness.

Her eyes harden. "Okay. Speak."

"Can I come in?" *Please.*

She watches me for far too long before shifting backward and opening the door enough for me to slip inside. I wander further into her room as she shuts the door.

"If you're here to shit on me again, at least let me put on different clothes," she mutters. I look at her outfit and immediately regret it.

She's wearing nothing but small sleep shorts and a tank top with straps too loose to carry the weight of her breasts. I gulp and quickly look away.

"I'm here to apologize, Gracie," I say on an exhale.

She makes a sound in the back of her throat that explains just how little she believes that. I can't blame her.

"Right. Let me guess, it was my brother that sent you? I'm surprised you're even here considering how badly I must creep you out. I wouldn't want to catch your heels under the toes of my shoes."

My stomach drops. "Shit, princess. Nobody made me come here. And I shouldn't have said that stuff to you. It was out of line."

She glowers at me. "Don't call me that. Actually, just don't call me *anything*. Get out of my room, and don't come back."

"Yeah, I'm not going to do that," I say. Her cheeks are flaming, and the only thing I want is to hold them in my palms and find out just how hot they feel. "We need to talk about this. I'm not leaving this resort with these feelings between us."

"That's only because you can't live with your guilt, Tyler. I don't want you to apologize just because you feel bad. I want you to apologize because you care about me and can't stand the thought of ever hurting me."

I scrape a hand through my hair. "Are those not the same? Fuck, Gracie. I don't know what I'm doing here, but I'm trying."

Sadness flashes across the blue pools of her eyes. Panic swells inside of me.

"No, Tyler. They're not the same thing. And honestly, I don't blame you for not knowing the difference. It goes beyond the scope of what you can give me emotionally."

I take a step toward her, my lungs tight. "What does that even mean?"

"It means that I thought I could handle being with you sexually, without any emotion behind it or promises of what comes next. But I can't. You were right, I am naïve. But only when it comes to you."

My heart stops. Or that's what it feels like, at least. I reach out a hand for her, but she takes a step back, evading my touch. Confusion is a blaring noise in my mind as I begin to wonder what this reaction I'm feeling means. What this anger and frustration means and why I want to scoop her up in my arms and hold her there.

"You knew who I was before we started this," is all I can say.

She nods, her bottom lip quivering. "You're right. And there's nothing we can do about it now but keep to the agreement you made with me the first time we slept together. This stops here. What happened at that restaurant only solidified why we could never bring this home with us."

I don't like hearing that, and I grow more frustrated with myself. I'm being handed an out, a clean break, and I'm second-guessing why I even laid down that rule in the beginning. It's stupid. Absolutely mind-boggling.

"We still have time. Our flight isn't until tomorrow." It comes out in a rush, leaving me no chance to stop myself.

"You're not hearing me, Tyler," she murmurs, her voice breaking. "It hurts me to only have you like this. I want more."

In a rush, I'm in front of her, my arms wrapped around her shoulders as I pull her into my chest. Her exhale is shaky.

"If this is the only time I let myself have you, I'm not walking away a day early." I'm too much of a selfish bastard. I could never deny that, especially when I know it will only make the separation harder on her. But we're already here. She's already in my arms, and after a lifetime of denying myself happiness, I don't want to miss this chance when it's right in front of me.

Gracie Hutton might be my blind spot, but right now, she's the only thing I can see.

"One last time, princess. Just one more time and we can forget this trip ever happened and go back to normal."

Her cheek slides across my chest, the material of my T-shirt becoming damp. "I don't know if I can."

"Please." It's a warbled plea. I'm panicking, suddenly swimming in the fear of watching her walk away.

She tips her head back and looks at me, our eyes catching. I can see every emotion written in hers and wish she could do the same with mine. If she knew that for the first time in years, I'm genuinely scared of something—of someone—maybe she would say yes. Maybe she would understand.

I skate my stare over her face before leaning in and brushing the tip of my nose against hers. She inhales. "Give us one more night. After that, move on with your life. Go find someone who can give you what I can't."

She answers me by covering my mouth with hers. I sigh into the kiss but don't break it. The last thing I want is to stop kissing her.

My heart shakes the chains around it as I pick her up and

carry her to the bed. Setting her down on the edge of it, I start to remove her clothes, starting with the top and then pulling down the shorts that I plan on tossing off the balcony after we're done.

She stays silent the entire time, watching with shy eyes as I finish and then step back, reaching behind my head and pulling my shirt off. My shorts and briefs come next.

As soon as I'm naked, she's moving back on the bed and laying her head on a cream-coloured pillow. I move over her, settling between her legs.

Gracie shudders beneath me when my fingers brush her nipples, circling them with the pad of my thumb. I watch them harden from my touch and swallow the lump in my throat.

"Tyler," she whimpers, arching her chest. I cover her breasts with my hands, loving the soft feel of them against the calloused palms.

I drag my cock along her sex, rock hard from our simple touching. Like me, she's already turned on. With every pass of me across her puffed lips, she gets slicker, and it becomes harder to avoid slipping inside.

"I know. I know, baby," I rasp.

It feels intense, like suffocating in open air. I want to rub at the ache in my chest, desperate to make it go away.

Her fingers find my hair, curling in the strands and using them as leverage to pull me close. "I need you inside of me."

I nod because I need the same thing. Reaching between us, I line myself up with her entrance and slowly push in, breaching her inner walls. She clenches around me, and I bite the inside of my cheek.

She whimpers, but it's a sound of pleasure, not pain. Her legs wrap around me, keeping me close, and when I pull out, she's reaching for me, like she can't stand even the slightest distance between us.

I don't say anything about it. Not when I understand exactly what she's feeling.

We move together in sync, our breathing matching and

touches just as needy. She's weaseling herself further into my chest with each thrust, and by the time she's crying out in release, my thoughts are poisoned with thoughts of keeping her with me after we're done.

Long after.

The headboard slams into the wall as I hit my high, releasing inside of her, the lack of condom becoming abundantly clear. It's the second time now I haven't wrapped it up, but after she told me she was on the pill and both of us were clean, I guess I just stopped thinking about condoms.

I can already feel her eyes burning into my face when I come back down to earth. Looking at her, I shake my head once, as if that will highlight her fears and press delete before they have a chance to solidify.

Gracie watches as I roll off her and onto my back, not making another move to get off the bed. She blinks before looking at the bathroom door, like she wants to go clean up but is too afraid of what she'll find when she comes out.

I slip my arm beneath my head and say, "If you want to go to the bathroom, go. I'll be here when you get back."

Her breath hitches. "What?"

My eyes soften. "Go."

"Okay. I'll be right back." With brief hesitation, she gets up and waddles to the door. I laugh, watching her ass shake as she walks like a penguin.

It's probably wrong to stay here. It's too early on the last full day of our trip. But I don't want to get up. I want to be the arms she crawls into when she comes back out.

So, despite the consequences, I wait.

14

Adam

Although it was difficult, taking time off from school was the right choice. Even if my grades are already less than ideal.

Kinesiology has never been my end goal, but it is a stepping stone. Owning my own business has always been my dream, and in a few months, it will finally become a reality.

As soon as I turn twenty-two, I get access to a hefty trust fund set up by my stick-up-the-ass lawyer parents. I've kept what I plan to do with that money a secret for the past few years—ever since I first stumbled upon the idea of owning my own hockey training facility—knowing full well they would never approve.

If they knew what I was planning on doing with the lump sum in that account, I would never see a penny of it, and that just won't do.

Instead, they think I'm going to use it to invest in their law firm.

I've never been more excited than I am just thinking about the horror they'll feel when I drop the bomb on them. It's karma in the purest form. After years of abandoning me and treating me like I'm less than, they'll finally feel even a sliver of the devastation that comes with being disappointed by family.

I grin to myself and, for the first time in a long time, feel peace while thinking of my parents.

It's our last night in Mexico, and we're all on the beach, sipping fruity drinks under the moon. The ocean laps at the shore and covers my toes before receding again. It's relaxing—a perfect getaway. Resting against my knees, I look at the people beside me and smile.

Oakley has Ava tucked between his knees in front of him and whispers something in her ear that I definitely don't want to know. She blushes and pinches him under the arm.

Tyler and Gracie are closer than they should be, but only if you're looking hard enough. Tyler is frowning at the ocean, almost oblivious to the slight tilt of his body toward our best friend's sister while said sister is sneaking him looks every two seconds.

The more I see those two together, the more I'm beginning to wonder if their relationship is as simple as I thought. My mind is working hard to figure out what exactly happened between them on this trip and how it's going to impact what happens when we get home.

Whatever it is, we'll all figure it out together. That's what family does. I've learned that the hard way.

Our serene moment comes to a screeching halt when a string of curse words comes flying from behind us. All five of us spin around, our eyes wide.

We must all notice the man charging toward me at the same time because I spot Oakley pushing Ava toward Tyler before rushing to his feet while Tyler shifts Gracie behind him. Seconds later, a body collides with mine, and the back of my head is hitting the sand.

The air is forced from my lungs, and I wheeze, "What the fuck?"

My attacker moves to straddle my waist, and before I have a chance to roll out of the way, he punches me square in the face.

Stars swim in the air above me as my eye starts to swell, tears flowing down my cheeks.

The man above me leans on my chest, and I start to shove at him. My head is ringing by the time he's pulled off me. I gulp lungfuls of air and close the eye that isn't already swollen shut.

"Who the fuck are you?" Tyler roars before a groan rings into the night.

"That fucker fucked my girl!"

I peek open my eye and get my first close-up of the guy. He can't be much taller than five foot seven, but he's decently buff. It makes sense as to why my eye is already swollen.

He's got shoulder-length blond hair and bright blue eyes that hold an innocence that makes me think he's younger than we are. There's anger in those eyes, though. The kind you usually find in the depths of a scorned woman's.

Oakley grabs him by the back of the neck and yanks him back when he tries to come at me again.

"Who's your girl?" I cough.

"Are you kidding? You don't even remember?" He bares his teeth like a wild animal.

"Just answer the question," Tyler snaps.

"You're going to have to get more specific. We've been here for a week," I add. In that week, I've only slept with two women, but he doesn't have to know that.

"Penny," he spits. I blink, my mouth pulling into a grimace. "Blonde, short, green eyes."

"Oh!" I nod. The woman I met zip-lining. "She told me she was on a girls' trip and newly single. I don't sleep with taken women, buddy."

He scoffs. "You're lying to make yourself look like less of a scumbag."

It's Ava that breaks into laughter. I look at her with a lopsided grin. "You have no idea what you're talking about. If Adam says she told him she was single, it means she told him she was single.

It looks like you need to clean your own house before coming into someone else's and saying it looks like shit."

Her buzz is obvious in the whacked-up analogy. Oakley must notice it, too, because he pulls her protectively into his side.

"We could press charges, you know?" Gracie asks, standing beside Tyler now, her arms crossed. "Not only did you give him a black eye, but you could have a concussion."

"What's your name?" Tyler asks when my attacker starts to get nervous and fights Oakley's grip on him.

He blanches. "No way I'm telling you."

Tyler laughs menacingly. "You don't really have a choice here."

I push up on my elbows and watch as Oakley switches his grip on the guy to one hand before starting to root through his pockets. He pulls out a wallet and opens it, sliding an ID out of the front slot.

"Royce Halton from California," he notes.

"A Cali boy. How unexpected," Tyler grunts.

Panic fills Royce's eyes, and I sigh. "Let him go, Lee. I don't think we need to worry about him knowing who you are, but in case he ever finds out, I don't want this shit on you."

"Okay, hand him to me, then. I don't give a fuck about that, Adam. Let me throw him in the ocean," Tyler says. He moves to stand in front of Royce and bends to look him in the eyes. "You can swim, right?"

"I second Tyler's proposal." Gracie straightens her back and tries to glower at Royce but fails. I chuckle.

"This isn't a debate, Gray. Although I appreciate the comradery," I say.

It takes way too long, but I somehow get myself up and out of the sand without help. My ribs ache from the hit they took, and my head pounds. I don't even want to think about my eye right now. At least until I get some ice on it.

"I don't want to spend our last night here dealing with this guy. Plus, a black eye is badass," I add, trying to sound as confident as I can.

I've never been a fighter, and even now, that hasn't changed. Tyler and Oakley do enough fighting for the three of us and then some.

"You want to let him off with the shit he just pulled?" Tyler asks, confused. He shakes his head. "You're a different breed, Adam."

Ava comes to my side and, with a firm hand, turns me to face her. She gives me a sympathetic smile before softly inspecting my eye.

"Fine. But if we see you again before we leave, you're going to walk away looking a lot worse than Adam. Am I clear?" Oakley asks Royce.

"Yeah. Shit, sorry." Royce takes off, his feet stomping in the sand.

Gracie blows out a breath. "What a dumbass."

"Let's make sure from now on you're being a bit more careful where you guys stick your dicks, yeah?" Oakley asks.

"Yeah, Dad. I promise," I tease. If there's anything that serves as a good reason for a bit of celibacy, it's being attacked by the boyfriend of a woman you thought was single.

Tyler doesn't say anything, and when I spare him a fleeting look, he's staring at his feet. I know right then my gut was right. His eyes lift—filled with both a dare and threat—and meet mine. I push away the discomfort in my stomach and nod in reassurance.

We'll talk about this when we get home.

Oakley

AVA NUZZLES her head beneath my chin as I pull the duvet over her bare back. She hums against my neck.

"I don't want to go back tomorrow."

I run my fingers through her hair and frown. "Me either."

Our first preseason game is next week, and after missing a couple of practices for this trip, I'm going to be stuck at the rink all day, every day, until then. The thought of being away from Ava for so long is nearly painful.

Living on the road is not easy, and yeah, it's what I've always wanted, but this part of the job is the hardest. In a perfect world, Ava would come with me wherever I went. But I would never ask that of her. I couldn't.

"Do you ever think about where we would be if I was never drafted?"

She pulls back and places a hand on my chest to balance herself upright. "Why? What's wrong?"

"Nothing, baby. I'm just thinking. As soon as we get back . . ."

"You'll be gone again?" she finishes for me. "I know. But you're doing what you love. That's enough for me. I didn't go into our relationship thinking you'd be glued to my side all the time, Oakley."

"We also didn't know I would be playing in Seattle."

Her brows scrunch. "Where is this coming from?"

"I don't know. I guess it's just been a mix of the off-season and being here that makes me miss when I didn't have to prepare for a time where I had to be away from you. It's only my second season, and I'm dreading leaving."

She nods, eyes soft. Her fingers brush back the hair flopping on my forehead. "You'll be home sometimes too. It's not like you're on the road for the entire season. We'll make the best of what we get. Just like we did last year."

"If I could give you every minute of every one of my days, I would. I hope you know that," I breathe, resting my forehead against hers.

This sentimental side of myself is one I never saw coming. But now that I've broken through that wall, there's no way I could ever rebuild it. Plus, Ava loves it. That in itself is well worth dealing with my teammates chirping at me for my cheeseball side every chance they get.

"I know. And I love you for that."

"Just for that?" I ask, one eyebrow lifted.

She rolls her eyes and lies back on my chest. I drop my hand to her side and start drawing lazy circles on her skin.

"Are you searching for compliments, Oakley Hutton?"

"From you? Always."

Her laugh is a shot of pure serotonin. "Keep rubbing my side like that and I'll tell you as many compliments as your heart desires."

"Before or after you fall asleep?"

"Mm, after?"

I kiss the top of her head and pull her tighter. "That's what I thought. I'll be waiting for my compliments tomorrow morning."

She hums something incoherent under her breath before falling silent. I lie beside her, awake and staring at the curve of her shoulder until the day catches up to me, and I drift off after her.

I'm half-asleep when I promise myself that I am going to do everything in my power to spend as many nights with this woman in my arms as I can.

Forever.

15

Tyler

The first thing I notice when I wake up is how cold I am. I rub my eyes and look at the window, expecting to find it open but seeing it closed instead.

No, the lack of warmth is because I'm alone. There isn't a smart-mouthed blonde in my bed, and for reasons beyond me, that upsets me. I kick off the blankets and get out of bed, pissed with myself.

"Get a grip," I mumble.

Bypassing the bathroom, I head right for the kitchen. I turn on the coffee pot and settle in front of the sink before turning on the tap and splashing cold water on my face.

We got back from Mexico yesterday, and despite what happened between us, I've been radio silent. Gracie has called twice and texted more times than I want to count, but I haven't been able to talk to her. Or more like I won't let myself talk to her.

The way I'm feeling right now is exactly why we need to leave what happened in Mexico *in* Mexico. Gracie Hutton has started to get in my head, and I have to throw her out before it's too late. Even if that hurts her. And me.

I curse under my breath when someone knocks at my front

door. Considering there are only a handful of people who know where I live, this can either be good or really bad.

With a groan, I grab a dishtowel from the counter and wipe off my face before throwing it back and heading for the door. The knocking continues until I unlock the door and whip it open.

Adam grins at me, two coffees in his hands. "Knock knock, motherfucker."

"What time is it?" I step to the side to let him in before closing the door. He walks inside and makes himself home on the couch.

"Ten. Here," he says, handing me a coffee. "You look like shit."

I glare at him but take the cup anyway. "Don't show up unannounced next time, and I'll try my hardest to look better for you."

"Thanks, babe. I didn't come here for pleasantries, though. Sorry to break it to you."

I sit beside him on the couch. "Good. I'm not in the mood."

He taps his fingers against his coffee cup and turns to me, all business. The swelling in his eye is still brutal, but it's nothing compared to the bruising.

"I let you get off the plane without asking because I knew you would lie to me in front of everyone else. But as your best friend, I'm asking now. You and little H? You slept together, right?"

"Shit," I mutter. My stomach twists.

"Yeah, I figured I was right. Now you need to explain to me how you were so fucking stupid before I do what Oakley is going to when he finds out about this," he says. The disappointment in his eyes has me looking away.

"He's not going to find out."

Adam lets out a brash laugh. "You have more screws loose than I thought if you think he's not going to eventually notice the same way I did that something is going on between you and his sister. You're lucky he was too love drunk on his own girl to pay much attention to the two of you miscreants."

"He won't notice because I'm putting a stop to it. We agreed before we even started anything that this wouldn't last past Mexico. I'm making good on it."

He looks doubtful. "Gracie agreed to that?"

"She was the one who said we needed to stop." And I ignored her and slept with her again anyway, blurring the lines she was trying to draw in the sand, and left her in the airport without a single answer to her questions.

"Huh."

"Huh?" I echo. "What the hell does that mean?"

"You're not blowing smoke up my ass right now?"

"No. What business do I have with an eighteen-year-old anyway? I'm sure if anyone else found out about this, they'd be calling me a fucking pervert right now."

"You're only three years older than her, but that's beside the point. The point is that you and Gray can't happen. It would ruin your relationship with Oakley. He would absolutely see it as a betrayal."

"I know that."

"So, you're really done?"

I swallow. "Yeah. It's done."

He narrows his eyes on me and searches my face for any hint that I'm lying. It's hard not to break under his stare, especially when I'm only telling half the truth.

I am done, but I don't want to be.

"I AM SO sorry I'm late, Gray. My lecture ran long, and there's this road closure over by the Starbucks that's blocking up the sidewalk, and I swear it would kill the guys filling up the potholes to actually move when someone says excuse me."

Ava blows out a breath and collapses in the chair across from me. I already ordered her some fruity drink the small restaurant has on special today, and before she's even situated, she's gulping it back.

I raise a brow, amused.

Her hair is curled in loose waves, and she's wearing a deep green turtleneck sweater that makes the green in her eyes pop, along with a two-piece gold necklace that I immediately love. She looks very professional but also cute. Like she's trying hard but not too hard. It's effortless beauty that only she can pull off.

Once she's drained the entirety of the odd, vase-shaped glass, she slides her purse off her shoulder and plops it on the table.

"Thirsty?" I giggle.

Her eyes twinkle when she smiles. "Parched. Thank you for ordering that for me, by the way. It's been a day."

"Wanna talk about it?"

"Is that why you asked me to meet you here today? To talk about *me*?" She looks unconvinced.

I fiddle with the tiny plastic straw in my virgin bellini and try to gain the courage to ask Ava for help.

Wait, plastic straw?

I know we should be saving the turtles one straw at a time, but I'm secretly happy this restaurant hasn't changed to paper ones yet. I've only been sitting here with my drink for a handful of minutes, but it would have been mush by now. Mushy paper straws are becoming my kryptonite.

Whatever, that's not important right now. What is important is grabbing the moment by my lady balls and telling my soon-to-be sister-in-law that I slept with my brother's best friend, and now I don't know what to do.

Good God. *I'm doomed.*

I'm relieved when Ava throws her hand up in front of her. "Actually. First, I need to ask if what you're about to tell me is something I'll have to keep from your brother. Because call it sisterly instinct, but I am pretty sure I know where this is going, and with that said, I can't keep secrets from Oakley. I just can't."

My shoulders fall. "Well, there goes that."

"Oh, Gracie. I'm right, aren't I?" she asks and exhales slowly when I nod. "Crap. I had a feeling something was going on, but I didn't think you guys would be that brave."

"Brave? Try stupid. Everything is ruined now."

"As opposed to how things were before?"

I sniff. "Yeah. Good point."

I fight the urge to check my phone in hopes that Tyler has finally returned one of my calls or texts. If he hasn't by now, he isn't going to at all. It's been a week of silence and crushed self-esteem.

His quick dismissal at the airport should have been a clear sign that whatever I felt between us that last time together wasn't real. He wanted sex badly enough he was willing to indulge me in an emotional fuck, that's all. So why am I still here wondering what it would take to get him to call me back?

I push aside my glass and drop my head in my hands. "There's something wrong with me, Ava. The part of my brain that's supposed to realize when I'm up against impossible odds is broken or maybe just not there at all. How many times can I be hurt by the same person before I finally close that door? God, how pathetic."

"Hey," she scolds, gently peeling my hands from my face. Her smile is sad. "Gracie Hutton and pathetic shouldn't even exist in the same universe, babe. Fuck any guy who makes you feel less than what you're worth."

"Ava, I did that already. That's how I got in this situation." I half laugh, half choke.

"You know what I mean. If this guy—I refuse to say his name out of respect for your brother—is too blind to see what's shining right in front of him, then he isn't worth it. When he realizes exactly what he lost, you'll be there grinning at the helpless look on his face. So will I."

"Hello, ladies. Are you ready to order?"

Ava nearly jumps out of her skin as the waiter appears seemingly out of nowhere, while my eyes bulge and my hand smacks the table.

"Do you not make any sound when you walk? Holy crap," Ava swears, a hand on her chest.

The waiter laughs, and I notice that he has a nice smile, like one you would see on a TV commercial promoting toothpaste. There's a beauty mark on his cheek that seems to be in the same place as a deep dimple. He's cute—the type of guy I would have been into two years ago.

Like I did when I first ordered our drinks, I realize how attractive he is. And it has the same effect on me now as it did then.

Said effect being *nothing*. Surprise, surprise, the Tyler curse is as strong as ever.

"My bad. I'm sorry, ladies." The waiter grins right at me, his eyes an intense shade of light blue that seems all wrong.

I muster up a smile, not wanting to come off as rude, but it's not very convincing. Ava clears her throat, finally capturing his attention.

"Maybe we'll just get some nachos. What do you say, Gracie?"

Her use of my name doesn't slip past me, and I glare at her.

The waiter—Phillip, according to the name written on the corner of his shirt—looks back at me now. He flashes me a lopsided grin and steps up closer to the table, as if he was invited.

"The nachos are one of my personal favourites," he says.

"Nachos are fine," I answer before bringing my cup back toward me and sucking back my drink.

"Great. I'll go ring that through for you."

"Yeah, great," I sigh when he spins around way too enthusiastically and jots away. "I don't want to be set up, Ava. I'm too jaded from one asshole to try and get with another."

"Hey, Phillip doesn't seem like an asshole."

I give her a pointed look. "Not the point. Now, are you going to give me advice, or do I need to expand my outreach and find someone else?"

Ava rolls her eyes. "Good luck. We both know I'm the only person you want to talk to about this, even if I shouldn't be."

"Okay, then tell me what to do, Oh Great One, because I'm losing my mind here. How do you move on from someone who has made it so abundantly clear they don't want you?"

Ava slouches in her seat and exhales a heavy breath. There's a kind of sympathy in her eyes that makes the hurt in my chest expand.

I barely catch the brief flicker of her eyes toward Phillip before she says, "You do the only thing you can do. Get over him by getting under someone else."

Tyler and Gracie's story continues in Blissful Hook, a full-length novel.

Available now on Amazon and Kindle Unlimited.

Thank you so much for reading Between Periods!

If you enjoyed this story, please consider leaving a review on Amazon or Goodreads. Reviews help authors more than you know!

Join my Facebook group, Hannah's Hottie's, and get all of the inside news before I post on my other social media accounts, and chat about all things books with other readers.

The Swift Hat-Trick Trilogy

Lucky Hit — Oakley and Ava
Between Periods
Blissful Hook — Tyler and Gracie
Overtime — Matt and Morgan
Vital Blindside — Adam and Scarlett

Amateurs In Love Series

Craving The Player — Braden and Sierra #1
Taming The Player — Braden and Sierra #2
Player Of Mine — Braden and Sierra books #1 & #2 combined in one duet edition.

Reading Order

Even though all of my books can be read on their own, they do all take place in the same universe and have multiple crossovers between characters. To avoid spoilers and to get the best reading experience, I have included a recommended reading order.

Lucky Hit — Oakley and Ava

Between Periods

Blissful Hook — Tyler and Gracie

Overtime — Matt and Morgan

Craving The Player — Braden and Sierra #1

Taming The Player — Braden and Sierra #2

Vital Blindside — Adam and Scarlett (Coming September 2022)

Blissful Hook

Everyone knew the rules.
Gracie Hutton was off limits.
But Tyler's never been one to follow rules.
And now she's about to become his ultimate sin.

Tyler Bateman doesn't know what easy means. He's never had an easy day in his damn life. Everything he has, he's worked for. Blood, sweat, and tears.

Hockey is his escape, a passion he never knew he could possess. He wants to succeed. He wants to prove that he's worth something.

He wasn't expecting her to matter. He didn't want her to. But she had other plans, and now his best friend's sister is about to ruin his life.

And he might just let her.

Vital Blindside

Adam White is many things, but a single dad was one he never saw himself becoming. He was twenty-three when the plan he had for his life crumbled at his feet. In the blink of an eye, he went from a flirtatious playboy just getting his new business up and off the ground to a struggling father of a two-year-old boy he never knew existed.

Yet somehow, Adam still accomplished what he thought was impossible. And ten years later, he doesn't think his life can get any better. His son is his world, and his business, White Ice Training, is one of the most popular hockey training facilities in Vancouver. But in the chaos of hiring a new trainer, he stumbles upon the name of a woman he would recognize anywhere. A woman he decides right then and there he'll do anything to convince to take the job.

One terrible game was all it took for Scarlett Carter to lose everything. After a career-ending injury destroys her chances of ever playing professional hockey again, she finds herself lost in a mess of guilt-stricken "what-ifs" and broken dreams. Moving back home to Vancouver was never in the playbook, but neither was letting herself get tricked into taking a job working for a man who seems to want to stop at nothing to see her forgive the sport that broke her.

Scarlett wants to forget the hockey world, but the single dad refuses to let her move on. And the more time she spends with

Adam, the harder she's finding it to resist him and the sly grins he seems to only give her. She can't help but wonder why he cares so much about her. And more importantly, why she can't bring herself to make him leave her alone.

Pre-order Now!

Acknowledgements

As soon as I finished this book, I was hit by a tsunami of different feelings, but the most prominent was overwhelming happiness. These characters are my first loves, the ones who started it all, and I am so excited to be sharing this novella with all of my readers.

I wouldn't even be here writing this story without the support and love that you, the readers, have shown these characters. And for that, I owe you the biggest thank you. Thank you for loving Oakley's lion's heart, Ava's gentle touch, Gracie's sassiness, Tyler's broken soul, and Adam's sunshine.

To my amazing group of beta and arc readers, you guys are my confidence and encouragement. Thank you for everything.

Thank you to Sandra, my editor, for cleaning up all of my messes and turning this manuscript into something worth publishing.

Thank you to the @booksnmoods team for creating this cover. I couldn't have asked for anything better.

Shelby, Mia, Hayley, and Becci, you are my girls. I will never be able to repay you for all of your love. I love and adore each of you.

About The Author

Hannah is a twenty-something-year-old indie author, mom, and wife from Canada. Obsessed with swoon-worthy romance, she decided to take a leap and try her hand at creating stories that will have you fanning your face and giggling in the most embarrassing way possible. Hopefully, that's exactly what her stories have done!

Hannah loves to hear from her readers and can be reached on any of her social media accounts.

Instagram : @hannahcowanauthor
Facebook/Twitter : @hannahdcowan
Facebook reader group : Hannah's Hotties
Website: hannahcowanauthor.com

Printed in Great Britain
by Amazon